S0-BEQ-823

SHADOWS

Only in the darkness was Julie Hobson
totally free. Only between twilight
and dawn could Julie express the passion
which was the deepest part of her nature.
And only those others who also came to
life at night accepted her—the cab
drivers, the streetwalkers, the abortionist,
the gay boys, the clandestine lovers, the
outcasts. Only they understood that she was
running and, like them, might one day be caught.

"Vivid life ... drama and suspense"
—Baltimore Evening Sun

"Sordid, realistic, and violent ...
Excellent novel ..."
—Durham Morning Herald

NIGHT STORY

BABS
H. DEAL

PAPERBACK LIBRARY, Inc.
New York

PAPERBACK LIBRARY EDITION

First Printing: September, 1963
Second Printing: October, 1965

This Paperback Library edition is
published by arrangement with
David McKay Company, Inc.

For ERIN DAVIS and PIXIE ALSPAUGH
  "A teacher affects eternity"

For ELIZABETH HAMMACK
  "One friend in a lifetime is much"

Library of Congress Catalogue Card Number:
  62-10752

The quotation on page 65 is from "A Fallen
Star," copyright 1957 by Tree Music, 319 7th
Avenue North, Nashville, Tennessee, written and composed by
James Joiner, 123 E. Alabama
Street, Florence, Alabama. Used by express
permission of the composer.

*Paperback Library books are published by Paperback
Library, Inc. Its trademark, consisting of the
words "Paperback Library" and associated distinctive
design, is registered in the United States Patent
Office. Printed in the United States of America,
Paperback Library, Inc. 260 Park Avenue South,
New York, N.Y. 10010.*

Everyone carries a shadow, and the less it is embodied in the individual's conscious life, the blacker and denser it is. We carry our past with us, to wit, the primitive and inferior man with his desires and emotions, and it is only with an enormous effort that we can detach ourselves from this burden.

—C. J. JUNG

No man can be redeemed from a sin he has not committed.

—Gnostic doctrine

Those who have reached the Stygian realm and returned are Orpheus, Hercules, Theseus, Ulysses, and Æneas. Also Persephone, who rules.

1.

"THERE comes Jackson Ferguson," Dupree Harris said. "I reckon it's night." He pushed himself away from the coffee urn behind the counter and went to the switch that controlled the neon sign in front of the Majestic Café.

Outside the shadows reached across the square, clutching the east side of the block. The street lights hadn't gone on yet, but the dusk had thickened in the corners. And along the street from the south Jackson Ferguson was coming with his slow walk, each foot planted firmly against the concrete, his blackjack slapping gently against his muscled leg.

Dupree threw the switch and the sidewalk outside turned red. Julie Hobson got up from the stool by the cash register and came to look out the window. "Look at him," she said. "He comes out at night like a ghoul. Ole Nightwalker Ferguson." She laughed. "This is the damnedest town, Harris. It chaosed me the first time I got a good look at it."

Dupree shifted the toothpick in his mouth and went back to the coffee urn. "Nobody paying you to stay here, is there?" he said.

Julie laughed again. "I wouldn't say that, old buddy," she said. "I'm probably a remittance man—woman—what have you."

The door opened and Will McCain came into the café, shutting the door behind him with a backward push of his body. He was short and muscular, with thick brown

7

hair and brown eyes of the type called moon eyes. When the light hit them they became opaque. He was seventeen years old but he looked older. That was his eyes too. He grinned at Julie. "Hi, beautiful," he said. "Keeping Dupree company while the wife's away?"

Dupree turned his back on him and drew a cup of coffee.

Will laughed. "You can get me one while you're at it," he said. "Had to get in here before ole Ferguson saw me. He'd probably want to know where I was going, here after dark." He sat down by Julie. "Why ain't you down at Machen's filling station, helping Arlie fill gas tanks?"

Julie raised one black eyebrow. "Why don't you ever keep your mouth shut?" she said.

"She don't like me, Dupree," Will said. "The only one of the McCains she likes is brother Carter. Carter, the Terrible, friend of man, defender of woman. Gimme some nickels." He shoved a quarter across the counter and stood drumming his hand on the plastic surface until Dupree pushed the nickels across to him. Laughing softly he walked over to the jukebox and leaned against it with both hands, peering at the cards inside.

Dupree watched him, then looked at Julie. "Will you tell me how he and Carter ever got to be brothers?" he said.

Julie shrugged. "Where is Carter, anyway?" she said. "He's usually in by this time."

Dupree looked carefully down at his hands. "He's running a little errand for me tonight," he said.

Will walked back from the jukebox. "You ain't got nothing fit to play on that damn box," he said. He turned to Julie. "Yeah, old Carter's off to Georgia with Dupree here's wife. Ain't you heard?" He put his hand on Julie's shoulder.

"Quit it," she said firmly. She stood up and moved away from him toward the door. She was a tall girl, with a firm big-boned body. She wore her hair high on her head in a mass of black curls. Her eyes were green, startling under black brows. "You talk too much," she said.

Will grinned at her. "Yeah. Carter's the silent member of our family. Got up tonight and ate breakfast like he was on his way to the chair. Says he's got a Georgia fare like it was a bodyguard job for the governor. I figured

8

he'd got into some trouble or other. But damned if I don't see him not thirty minutes later picking up Mrs. Harris at her house, her all dolled up. You know about it, Dupree?"

"Knock it off, Will," Dupree said. "You don't hurt anybody with your big-mouthing but Will McCain."

"O.K.," Will said. "Be one all your life. You want to take a ride around the block, sugar?"

"How?" Julie said. "Piggy back?"

"Why I figured we'd borrow a car off Arlie if you're too good to ride in my pickup. If he thought you wanted it, he'd be damned sure to accommodate you."

"And he'd damn well be the only one to accommodate me," Julie said.

"Well now," Will said. "Who'd have thought it. Arlie Machen making out with the town's untouchable."

"Can it, Will," Dupree said.

The door opened. "Cheese it," Will said loudly in Julie's ear. "It's Blackjack Ferguson, the pride of Maynard County." He brushed by Ferguson and went out the door.

It was night now. The street lights had come on and the street shone blue and artificial through the glass front of the café. Jackson Ferguson sat down on a stool and Dupree silently served him a cup of coffee. Julie sat smoking, her eyes fixed on the windows.

The deputy didn't speak either. He drank his coffee, looking into the cup between swallows. He was tall, with gray hair and round steel-rimmed glasses. His hands were long-fingered, slim—the hands of an artist. They curled tightly around the white china mug. He finished the coffee and pushed the cup away from him. He stood up, looking at Julie. She looked coolly back at him, and he turned away, looking up at the illuminated clock over the doorway. He took a nickel from his pocket and looked carefully at it.

"Gimme some cigarette papers," he said.

Dupree took them from the glass case and Ferguson put the nickel on the counter. Dupree handed him the small package. "Don't I get no change?" Ferguson said.

"You know they've gone up," Dupree said. The words had the sound of a ritual. It was natural they should; Dupree had been saying them every night for a good long while now.

9

"Like everything else," Ferguson said. He selected a toothpick carefully from the glass jar on the counter and went out the door. Through the window they could see him in the red glare of neon, slowly beginning his walk down the north side of the square. He would walk it in measured strides, turn, walk down the west side, turn again, go up the south side, turn, walk up the east side, turn, and return. Each hour he would stop for coffee.

Julie banged on the counter with her hand. "Set up the coffee, Harris," she said loudly. "The shadow has departed for an hour. Eat, drink, and be merry. Do you really give him all that coffee?"

Dupree shrugged. "He's The Law." He looked up at the clock and wiped his hand across his forehead.

Julie looked at him. "What's the trouble, Dupree?" she said. "Where's Carter taking Estelle?"

He shook his head. "Just over to Georgia. They'll be back another couple hours most likely. It's a good clear night. Make good time over the mountain."

"O.K.," Julie said. "I won't say anything else." She looked around. "Where the hell is everybody tonight?"

"Ain't really suppertime yet," Dupree said. "They'll be coming in. It's always later in summer. Specially in August. They have to wait for night to come on good before they can think about food. Here comes ole Jake now. Course, he ain't interested in food." He laughed.

Jake came in the door, smiling broadly, wearing the battered hat and neatly pressed suit he always wore. When he saw Julie he pranced over to her, his smile becoming even more broad. "Here she is," he said. "The true nocturnal creature. Miss Hobson in her habitat of night. What you doing in Bellefonte anyway, girl? You don't belong here."

Julie smiled at him. She was fond of Jake and she made her usual answer to him. "I like it here, Jake," she said. "This town really gives me a blast."

A lot of people wondered what Julie was doing in Bellefonte, but Jake McCain was the only one who ever asked her. Even Arlie Machen, who had come closer to knowing her than anyone else in town, didn't know.

She came to Bellefonte one night in winter on the twelve-o'clock bus. The twelve-o'clock bus made connections from all points north and told them nothing. Carter

10

McCain saw her get off the bus carrying one suitcase and a small leather case and walk down Railroad Street toward the tracks. He leaned out of the car window and asked if she wanted a taxi but she shook her head and went on, turning her coat collar up around her neck. She walked down Railroad to the tracks and over them and across, disappearing in the cold midnight air. Later they knew she was staying with an old couple who lived in one of the half-dozen houses for whites on that side of the tracks, a Mr. and Mrs. Riley, retired railroaders who lived alone and in isolation, coming out to tend their small garden or purchase a few groceries from the Negro store at the end of the street. She had a room with them, whether rented or as a guest there no one knew. Later too they knew she didn't work and that she wasn't anybody's girl. Not until Arlie started seeing her. There was a feeling that some night she would be moving on. But it wasn't yet.

"You seen Carter around?" Jake said.

"He's on an out-of-town fare, I think," Julie said. "You need him for something?"

Jake shook his head. "No. Just wanted to see him. Only damned member of my family fit to talk to. Thought he might be in to eat."

"He's gone somewhere for me," Dupree said.

"Oh, hiddy, Dupree. Where's your beautiful wife?"

"Gone with Carter," Dupree said. "They had to pick up some things over in Georgia."

"Ain't quite so cheery around here without her," Jake said. "She is sure one good-looking little girl. How'd you ever get her?"

Dupree smiled. He leaned over the counter and winked at Julie. "Well, Jake," he said. "You might say I found her. Went up to ole man Clopton's house on the Old Road to Lansford one day to see about buying a pig. And there she was, sitting on the porch shelling peas . . . shelling about one pod every thirty minutes and looking off at the road. Just waiting. So I brought her to town."

Jake laughed. "Just sitting there waiting for Dupree Harris to make up his mind to buy a pig off her daddy," he said. "Can you beat it? And damned if she don't look like something off Fifth Avenue in New York. Went to buy a pig off her daddy. God, You move in mysterious

11

ways." He sat down on a stool. "Give me a clean glass," he said. "That calls for a tetch."

Dupree looked up at the clock.

"He's still over on the south side," Jake said. "Besides, I'll keep it under the counter."

Harris pushed the glass over and Jake filled it from a bottle he took out of his pocket. "Will you join me, Miss Hobson?" he said.

Julie shook her head. "Too early for me. I've still got to eat something."

"Food," Jake said. "Jesus." He drank from the glass.

Jake McCain was a philosopher, or the nearest to one Bellefonte, Alabama, had ever produced. He was the brother of the most prosperous bootlegger in the county, but he didn't bootleg. He drank. He'd drunk most of his life, but there had been a time when he worked in the daytime. That was before he was forty years old. When he became forty he walked into the sawmill where he had worked for twenty-two years and quit. He hadn't worked since. He began to sleep in the daytime and stay up and talk and drink at night, which was, he said, the way man was meant to do in the first place. Nobody was sure how he lived. His wife had long since left him, gone back to her family, and he had no children. He lived in a room over the gas station on the north end of the square. The building was owned by Arlie Machen but if somebody else paid the rent for Jake, Arlie never talked about it. Arlie never talked much about anything. Jake had lived a frugal life in his days at the sawmill and most people figured he'd been quietly putting by something to live on for the time when he quit, but no one knew that for sure either. They accepted Jake and the life he lived, as they did many of the things in Bellefonte, as part of the pattern.

People had begun to come into the café now: two salesmen who were staying at the hotel where the food was bland if nutritious, the owner of the pool hall, the ticket agent from the railroad. Dupree filled a row of glasses with cold water and picked up his pencil and pad.

"You want me to give you a hand?" Julie said.

Dupree looked at her. "Hell, no," he said. "You're all dressed up."

She shrugged. "It cleans."

"Nope. I've swung it by myself before." He went over to the booths along the opposite wall.

The wall fans blew air into the room, but the heat was oppressive now that the place was full of people. Julie pushed her hair back and propped her fist on her chin. The door opened again and Arlie Machen came into the lights. He was a tall man, muscular and handsome. He moved silently and softly. He was dressed in khaki. He walked over to Julie and put his hand on her hair briefly before sitting down. "Hi," he said.

"Hello, lover."

"Dupree got his tail in a crack?" he said. "I'll get my own coffee. Want some?"

She nodded and he went around behind the counter and drew coffee from one of the urns.

"Mr. Machen," Jake said. His glass was empty and he had pushed his hat back on his head. "How's the gas and oil business tonight?"

"Slow," Arlie said. "Like always." He came back around the counter. "Probably close up around twelve-thirty or so. Want to go somewhere?"

"Always ready to go somewhere," Julie said. "Where?"

"I don't know. The Line maybe. Too late for Hunter City."

"Anywhere," Julie said. "I'd just as soon sit on the square and hoist a few myself."

"And get hoisted into the county jail," Arlie said.

"Ole Blackjack don't scare this one," Julie said.

"Is there anything that does?" Arlie said.

"Yeah," Julie said. "The thought of spending the rest of my life watching that one stalk around this block every night. It scares me silly. Doesn't it you?"

Arlie looked into her eyes for a moment. "I reckon it could," he said. "But I don't let it." He drank from his mug. "You seen Carter around?" he said.

Julie shook her head. "He's over in Georgia doing something for Dupree."

"Thought he might want to have a few with us tonight," Arlie said. "After he makes the late train."

"Maybe," Julie said. "And maybe he'll have a date. We haven't been seeing much of him lately."

Arlie looked at her. "You got something against his girl?" he said.

13

"No. I sort of like her. But she's not for Carter. Take a good look at her sometime, Arlie. She is definitely not for Carter."

"You taken him to raise or something?" Arlie said.

"Oh, hell," Julie said shortly. "You know everybody likes Carter. He's your best friend. That's the only interest I have in him."

"I'm hungry," Arlie said. "Wonder if Dupree'd mind if I just dished it up myself."

"Have a drink," Jake said.

They had forgotten him. He still sat on the stool watching them with interest. "Who is it my nephew dates?" he said.

"Carter?" Arlie said. "Why, Laura Lee Colvin."

"Jesus!" Jake said. "Irene Colvin's little girl? I thought she wasn't more than a baby. But then don't reckon I feel like Carter is either for that matter. Wonder what Irene thinks of it?"

Julie laughed harshly. "You know damned well what she thinks of it," she said. "You can see for yourself what Carter looks like."

"Don't be catty," Arlie said. He drained his coffee mug and handed it to Jake. "Pour one, Uncle Jake," he said.

"I'm not being catty," Julie said. "But you know and I know that Irene Colvin has an eye for good-looking boys. Not that I exactly blame her, considering her husband. Still, it don't bode well for Carter and his ladylove. And that, pet, is just what little Laura Lee is a ladylove. Like in the tales of old. I can imagine Carter wearing her scarf tied on his radiator cap, can't you?"

"What in the hell are you talking about?" Arlie said.

"Nothing," Julie said. "Pour me one too, Uncle Jake." She handed her mug across Arlie.

Dupree came back around the counter and began dishing up orders. "What you want, Arlie?" he said.

"Well," Arlie said. "I had planned on eating supper, but I've gotten onto the liquid refreshments now and I'm not so sure."

"How about a steak?" Dupree said.

"That's an idea."

"Put two on," Julie said. "We might as well get a good lining in our stomachs."

Outside, Jackson Ferguson had completed his first circuit of the block. He stopped in front of the café and looked at his watch. He'd have time to make another one. The picture show was letting out between features and there were groups of boys standing around in front of it. He planted his pistol more firmly on his hip and started around the square again.

"I don't think there's any need of me going in with you, is there?" Carter McCain said to the girl beside him.

"Yes you are too," Estelle Harris said. "You don't think I'd go by myself?"

She was a dark girl with wide brown eyes and a patrician nose that contrasted with her full, too-wide mouth. She wore her hair long, which emphasized her smallness. "You just say you're my husband. You'll probably have to sign something, I've heard."

"I don't want to do that," Carter said.

"You promised Dupree," Estelle said, pouting.

"Are you scared?" Carter said.

"Yeah. Sort of. I mean like going to the dentist, scared. But not as scared as I'd be not to. That's for sure. Come on now, Carter. You got to go in with me."

"O.K. Let me have a cigarette first." He reached behind the sun visor for the pack. "You want one?"

"All right." She accepted the cigarette and sat smoking, looking out the window at the white bungalow with the porch swing and the potted plants on the banisters. "It don't look like the kind of place it is," she said finally.

Carter laughed. "You expect them to advertise?" he said.

He was embarrassed and unhappy but he had accepted the commission for Dupree and he couldn't get out of it. The only thing he knew to do was see it through and get home quick. It wasn't really any concern of his anyway. He had no right or reason to make judgments. It was a favor he was doing for a friend and for a few bucks, and that was all. But he hated it anyway.

He looked at Estelle beside him, pretty, vain, irresponsible, and he tried to think of Laura Lee. But the image wouldn't come to him. Laura Lee didn't belong here. But he did. This was a place where Carter McCain would logically find himself. And it was no sort of place for Laura Lee to ever be. It scared him, thinking like that. It

15

put something between him and Laura Lee that he didn't want to see. It put him squarely where he belonged, on the night side of the world, and left Laura Lee where she belonged, in the daylight. That was how he always thought of her anyway. The small blonde image was always surrounded by sunlight in his mind. And that was very odd because he didn't think he'd ever seen her in sunlight. He didn't live in sunlight himself. When the sun was up he slept, when the lights came on in the darkness his day began. It was like that for him and for his family and for all his friends. They belonged to the night just like ole Blackjack Ferguson did. Although the day people might collide with them in the hours between dark and midnight there were the long stretches of daytime that belonged only to them just as there was the dense stretch of midnight to dawn that belonged to him and his kind. The meeting place wasn't enough to change that.

He watched the smoke on his cigarette, trying to eke it out, make it last a little longer. Being of the night was more than just a matter of employment. There were certain people who had to be that way. That was why they worked at night. Dupree and Estelle and their all-night café, Arlie Machen and his filling station, Ferguson, the other taxi drivers, his parents with their whiskey. And the others, those who didn't work at night at all, but lived that way all the same: his Uncle Jake and Julie Hobson. They could have slept at night and lived in the sun, but they didn't want to. And what did Laura Lee really want? He didn't know.

"You ready?" Estelle said.

"All right." He got out of the car and stretched, feeling his body taut after the long drive. It was a good body, and it behaved well for him. He was a little too thin, maybe, but the muscle was all right. "Come on," he said. "Let's get it over with."

The door was bare and plain, an ordinary door. He knocked and a Negro woman answered it and called over her shoulder. "Miz Myerson. These folks here."

Mrs. Myerson came out of the living room. She looked like somebody's mother or grandmother, a fat placid woman with short gray hair and a pleasant face. "You the folks from Alabama?" she said.

"That's right," Carter said.

Beside him Estelle seemed to have lost some of her nonchalance. Carter put a hand on her shoulder and patted her. He felt very out of place.

"Sit down, please," Mrs. Myerson said. She walked over to the door and flipped the night latch on. "That's all, Gertrude," she said to the colored woman. Then she motioned them in front of her through an archway into the living room. She sat down in an old-fashioned rocking chair and folded her hands across her stomach. "You the husband?" she said.

"Yes," Carter said.

"All right. I want to talk to her by herself first," she said.

"No," Estelle said.

She looked at her. "All right. I always ask if you're sure you want to go through with this before I do it. Are you sure?"

Estelle whimpered suddenly, a small sound, lost in the creaking rockers. Then she cleared her throat. "I'm sure," she said.

"It'll be two hundred dollars—cash," the woman said.

Estelle opened her pocketbook, a tooled leather box with fringed edges. She fumbled in it for a moment and took out a billfold fat with snapshots. She took out the two hundred dollars in twenty-dollar bills and handed it to the woman. Mrs. Myerson took the money and went to a big businesslike desk flanked by steel filing cabinets. She took a blank form out of a drawer and handed it to Carter. "Both of you sign it. Right there," she said.

Carter read the small printed form. It stated that the undersigned came here of their own accord and agreed to say nothing of the matter. He signed, watching his hand make the letters Dupree Harris in mild surprise. Estelle signed it quickly without reading it.

"You go on out on the side porch there," the woman said. She patted Estelle's shoulder and pushed her toward a door that led to the back of the house. Carter went to the porch. He was glad to get there. There were potted plants here too and a glider. He sad down, wondering how long it would take.

It didn't take long. In what seemed only a few minutes Estelle was standing in the door looking at him. She was

17

very pale, her face drawn a little. "Let's get out of here," she said.

"Are you all right?"

She nodded. "Fine. My ears sort of ring. That's all. You come on now, Carter. I don't like it here. I want to go home."

"All right."

Mrs. Myerson was standing by the front door, holding it open. She had a prescription blank in her hand and she handed it to Carter. "You can get this in the drugstore next door," she said. "It's just something to keep her from feeling sick at her stomach. That's all I can get you. If she needs something later I've already told her to try whiskey. Keep her walking. Don't let her go to bed. You hear me?"

"All right," Carter said.

"She told me that," Estelle said. "Come on. I want to get out of here." She went out the door and he followed her. She got in the car and slammed the door behind her. Carter went around and got in under the wheel. "We better go next door here and get this for you," he said.

"All right." She was sitting quiet, her eyes shut, something clutched in her hand. Carter looked down. It was her pants, white with lace on them. It made him feel terrible. He swallowed.

"Estelle," he said. "I wish Dupree was here."

She shook her head, her eyes still tightly closed. "I don't want him here," she said. "He hates me enough for doing it. He'd never forgive me if he'd come with me."

Carter looked away from her. He backed the car out and drove the few yards to the drugstore. "You want to come in?" he said.

"Yes. Wait a minute." She bent over and eased the pants over her feet and up her legs underneath her skirt. Carter looked carefully away from her.

"I can go in and get it," he said.

"I'm coming." She opened her door and got out.

The drugstore was dim and cool. There were marble-topped tables and old-fashioned wire chairs and a tall marble counter. There was no one in the store except the druggist, a round bald man with rimless glasses. They sat down at a table and he came over. Carter handed him the prescription.

Estelle sat very still, her hands still clenched. "Estelle,"

18

Carter said. "Are you sure you're all right? We got to drive back. Maybe I ought to get you to a doctor."

"Don't be an ass," she said shortly. "I'm perfectly all right. There wasn't anything to it. It didn't hurt at all, in spite of all those things they say. I just feel sick. Sick to my stomach." She stopped and looked at Carter. "And awful. Awful. Awful. Awful. Nothing feels real and I feel dirty. There. Now shut up."

Carter looked away from her. The druggist came over with a paper cup and a small bottle. "Five bucks," he said to Carter.

Carter took the money out of his pocket and handed it to him while Estelle was still fumbling with the leather bag. The druggist grinned. Carter stared hard at him. "Bring us two cups of coffee, you s.o.b.," he said.

The druggist shrugged and walked back to the counter.

Carter leaned over and sniffed the cup. It was ordinary spirits of ammonia. "Drink it down," he said. "It won't hurt and, who knows, it might even help."

Estelle drank obediently. He looked at the bottle. Ordinary paregoric. He laughed. "They don't plan on helping you out any, do they?" he said.

"What?" Estelle focused her eyes on him. They looked bright, yet fuzzy.

"Forget it," he said. "Here's the coffee." He drank both cups because she said she couldn't drink any. Then they walked out to the car and started home.

"You want to lie down in the back seat?" Carter said.

She shook her head. "She said not to lie down and go to sleep," she said. "I feel sort of lightheaded. Turn on the radio."

"All right." He flipped the dial and the car was filled with hillbilly music. He cut down the volume. "I'll have you home in no time," he said.

"I wish you wouldn't," she said softly. "I wish we could just ride on and on and on in the night, and never get back to that damned café."

"I know a bootlegger in the next town," Carter said. "We'll stop and get you some whiskey."

"That's a good idea. I could use it."

Carter didn't answer her, concentrating on the road in front of him. He was a good driver and he was in this moment damned glad of it. He felt a little sick himself.

In the next town he stopped at a café on the outskirts and went in. He bought a pint of Seagram's and brought it back and dumped it in Estelle's lap. She broke the seal with one of her long red nails and screwed the top off. "Want one?" she said.

He shook his head. "I sure don't want to lose my license tonight," he said.

"Poor Carter," she said, laughing. "You have got a carload of trouble, haven't you? You shouldn't be so damned good to people. This is what it gets you into. You hate it, you't you? You're just like Dupree. You can't see why on earth I don't want a drooling, sloppy baby slung on one hip while I dish hash with the other hand. Poor Carter. You'd probably feel better about it if I wasn't married."

He didn't answer her, but she was right. He would feel better about it if she wasn't married. There were times when people got themselves into something they had to get out of, but this wasn't one of them. Estelle had a husband who was nuts about her. One who had taken her off a back-country farm and who spent most of his money for clothes to put on her back. He tried again to think of Laura Lee, but the image blurred. "We're making good time," he said.

Estelle tilted the bottle up again. "Maybe I wouldn't have if it had been yours," she said.

He didn't answer her.

"You hear me?" she said.

"I heard you."

"Well?"

"You're tight."

"O.K.," she said. "So I am. But it's true. Though, come to think of it, Will is probably more my type. He looks some like you, but he don't have so many . . . so many what?"

"Scruples?"

"That's it. Scruples. Isn't that a word?" She giggled.

"You better save some of that," Carter said. "You might need it later."

"Sure." She screwed the top on the bottle and put it in her purse.

Going up the mountain out of Fort Morgan he heard her begin to cry. He drove on up the mountain, going as fast as he dared in the darkness. When he got to the drive-in at the top of the climb he pulled in behind the building and switched off the lights. "O.K., honey," he said. "Bawl." He took a handkerchief out of his pocket, looked at it, and put it back. "You got a handkerchief?" he said.

She nodded, fumbling in her purse. He let her cry for a few minutes. Then he went in and got some coffee and ice cream.

She sat up straight when he came back to the car and smiled at him. He handed her the carton of ice cream and she ate eagerly, sniffing occasionally. Then she managed some of the coffee.

Carter stood outside the car, drinking his coffee and looking at the lights of the drive-in.

Estelle leaned over and stuck her head out of the door on his side. "I'm sorry I was so bitchy, Carter," she said. "It's sort of a spooky feeling I've got. I didn't mean to take it out on you."

"Forget it. You through?" She nodded. He tossed the cartons out on the gravel and pulled back on the road. "I got to get you home before Dupree goes nuts," he said.

"All right." She leaned back against the seat and closed her eyes.

From where he sat in the shadow of the green ivy J. O. Colvin could see night come onto his street. He could watch the light come on at the corner, throwing the intersection into a bright hard glare. He could see the lights go on one by one in the Mayhill apartments down the street, and far away across the Johnsons' lot the cluster of lights from the railroad shacks. He did not look down the street toward town, because there he would see the glare of light from the service station on the corner, the first blight that had come on the street of home. It was not the only blight there now. Farther up the street past the Mayhills' was a new glass-and-concrete supermarket, blinking onto its concrete apron, the asinine pig face smiling down benignly from its round blue sign. There was a Ford agency too, full of fast, sleek, chromed machines, sitting in splendor on their own concrete behind plate-glass windows.

He did not like to think of any of these things on his street. It had been his street long before it became the highway. He remembered the days of dust and weed-choked wayside ditches. He remembered the time when there were only well-kept white houses here.

He was old. He felt old now and the lights from the service station made him sad, just as the smell of gasoline did in the dusk, and the sound of tires on the hard black pavements. He leaned back in his chair and listened to the creak the rockers made. That hadn't changed at all. That was the same as when his father had rocked on the wooden porch and when he had first inherited the rocker with the house.

His daughter came out the screen door, standing for a moment silhouetted against the hanging bulb inside the front hall. "Papa," she said. "You want some ice tea?"

"Not right now, I reckon," he said. "Sit down a spell."

"The dishes aren't done," she said. "I've got to help Mama."

"You work all day," J.O. said. "Sit down."

She came forward out of the light and sat down on the porch swing. "It sure is hot," she said tiredly. "Working in that air-conditioned office all day makes this old house a steam bath at night."

"You oughtn't be working," J.O. said comfortably. He rocked back and forth.

Laura Lee sighed. She still couldn't help feeling exasperation with her father, even though she knew that his mental blindness was involuntary, a part of him as much as his premature oldness, his shock of white hair. He simply did not believe there wasn't any money. It was no use trying to make him see the condition of the house, the rotting back porch, the peeling plaster, the musty living room. To J.O. it looked as it had in his father's day. There was no use explaining to him either that there was no meat in the smokehouse, that even the smokehouse had long ago ceased to be, sold off with the back lot to make way for a new brick office for a chiropractor. There were no chiropractors in J. O. Colvin's world.

He was a gentleman. Gentlemen did not work. They sat on the porch on a summer evening and watched the lights come on. They walked down for the mail in the brightness of morning and stood talking near the Sulphur Well with others of their kind. They took an afternoon nap after a cooling lunch and they walked back to town in the twilight to watch the day end.

Laura Lee supported her mother and father. She worked in the county agent's office, typing reports and filing complaints. She had gone away to college once—for a year, with the money from her grandmother's estate. But by the time Laura Lee was ready for college the money wasn't enough for more than a year. There had been the chance at a scholarship, but the night before she was to take the exam there had been a phone call from her mother. Laura Lee had come home and gone to work.

"No," J.O. mused. "Your place is at home. That's where J.O. Jr.'s is too. He's got no business off up north doing whatever it is he does up there. Sonny Colvin has got no business among the Yankees. He ought to come home."

"Yes, Papa," Laura Lee said. This was old stuff too, the waiting for Sonny to come home. He can wait on that forever, Laura Lee thought angrily. When Sonny left here he left. Oh, there were the money orders, those convenient money orders that were just big enough to make Irene exclaim and to make Laura's weekly check look even smaller than it was. Those money orders that came just seldom enough and irregularly enough so that her job was what fed them and fixed the worst of the leaks and put clean oilcloth on the kitchen table. Sonny's money went for clothes for Irene, or for a shiny new appliance that they could just as well have done without; or for steak dinners at the Majestic Café, or bootleg whiskey from Carter's daddy's.

She thought of Carter with longing, shutting her eyes to bring his face into focus in her mind, his eyes brown and yellow like a cat's, his nose thin and a little sharp, his mouth with its full lip, the front tooth that was chipped a little so that when she kissed him . . . She stood up. "I have to finish helping Mama," she said.

"You going out tonight, baby?" J.O. said.

"Yessir. Later."

"Some nice boy?"

"Of course, Papa." She laughed, turning her back on him. By nice he meant with money and blood. She wondered as she always did how he missed seeing the light on the taxi when Carter picked her up. Maybe he did and thought she was taking a cab to her assignations. She'd never hidden the fact that she dated Carter McCain but she'd never volunteered the information. She never would.

The kitchen was dark and hot. Irene Colvin stood in front of the old-fashioned sink that was so low you had to stoop to get to the dishpan. She had on a pair of slacks with a towel pinned around her waist. A cigarette dangled from the corner of her mouth. She was tall and thin, with a sharp, discontented face. Her hair, beginning to gray, was dyed auburn and her brows were plucked to a thin black line. Underneath the makeup the bones were still good. It was as though if you could only look hard enough you might surprise the beauty she once had been. "What the hell are you doing?" she said when Laura Lee came into the room. "You scared me. You sneak around like a cat."

Laura Lee shrugged. She picked up a dish towel and began drying the plates.

"You going out again tonight?" Irene said.

"Yessum."

"That McCain boy?"

"Yessum."

Irene looked at her closely. "You in love with him?" she said.

"Maybe."

"Your daddy'd die before he'd see you married to the bootlegger's son. You know that, don't you?"

"He's got to die sometime," Laura Lee said.

"My God," Irene said. "You sound hard."

"I don't get much chance to sound any other way around here."

"Now I reckon you're going to bring up that you didn't get to finish college," Irene said. She slapped the wet dishcloth over the top of the kitchen table.

"I'm not going to bring up anything," Laura Lee said. "I just get tired of listening to him sitting out there telling me I don't have to work."

Irene laughed. "Well, I can't say you make much," she said. She sat down on a kitchen chair and drew on her cigarette.

Laura Lee went on drying the dishes. "What'd you do with my new earrings?" she said.

Irene looked down at her shoes. "Well, I lost one of them," she said. "I'm sorry. It was the other night when I went over to talk to Sue Mayhill. I just couldn't find it anywhere. I went back and looked, but . . ."

"O.K.," Laura Lee said. "O.K." She slammed the silver into the table drawer and slammed the drawer shut.

"What you gonna wear tonight, honey?" Irene said.

"That white dress. It's the only thing I've got ironed."

"I don't think that looks so good on you," Irene said. "It's sort of young, don't you think?"

"Carter likes it," Laura Lee said.

"Oh, well," Irene said. "I suppose that's all that counts."

"That's all. Do you think there's any hot water left?"

"I don't know. It was running sort of cold that last skillet I did."

"Mama, if you'd use a pan of rinse water instead of holding them under the faucet . . ."

"It's so much trouble."

"So's heating water," Laura Lee said. She took two pans from the cabinet and filled them at the sink. Then she put them on the stove and turned the eyes on. The new electric stove and refrigerator represented two of Sonny's money orders.

"Maybe we can get a new water heater the next time Sonny . . ."

"We're going to put some of that up next time," Laura Lee said. "And we're going to fix the bathroom floor before the whole thing falls through onto the back porch."

"All right," Irene said. "You were the one wanting hot water." She lit another cigarette from the stub of the one she was smoking. "What do you and Carter do?" she said.

"Do?"

"On dates," Irene said. "Surely you do something."

"Yeah," Laura Lee said. "We go down to the Majestic Café and listen to the jukebox, we go to The Line and drink beer, we talk to Arlie Machen and Julie Hobson. And so on . . ."

"He looks a little rough to me," Irene said.

Laura Lee poured coffee from the pot on the stove and sat down across the table from her mother. "He isn't," she said shortly.

"Well, he's good-looking. I will say that for him," Irene said.

"He suits me," Laura Lee said. She drained her cup and picked up a pan of water from the stove. "If you hear a great big noise it's me, falling downstairs and scalding myself," she said as she went out the door.

Upstairs in the bathroom she set the pan of steaming water on the edge of the tub and leaned over to put in the stopper, feeling wet hot steam against her flushed face. Damn it, she thought, pouring the water. There goes any curl left in my hair. She went down for the second pan. Her mother still sat at the table, looking blankly into the coffee cup. She carried the second pan up the dark stairway and poured that into the tub. Then she put in cold water and mixed it, watching the swirl of water in the round-bottomed tub. The bathroom was in what had once been an old storeroom built out over the back porch. In the winter it was icy, the cold coming in from all directions. In the summer it was damp. Laura Lee could remember when it had been a new tight room, shored up and plastered over inside with beaverboard and painted a happy pink. Now the beaverboard sagged inward from the scantlings and the makeshift ceiling bowed downward, occasionally depositing dirt and debris from the rafters above into the bathtub. The floor, green pine to begin with, was rotting around the heavy fixtures.

When they were children Laura Lee and Sonny used to play hide-and-seek all through the big house and her favorite place to hide had always been the big pink wicker hamper in the corner. Sonny always got mad about it. He'd say, What's the fun if I know where you are every time? That was Sonny. He wanted things to be difficult and exciting and different every time around.

Laura Lee stepped into the tub. The water felt only lukewarm now. She sighed again. She wondered what Sonny did in New England. It seemed such an odd place for him to be. She always thought of New England as neat and white like a Christmas card or neat and green like an Easter card. She couldn't see Sonny in that neat setting, not small wiry Sonny with his black eyes and quick way of moving that made his slow way of talking seem even slower.

He'd been home once: the time he'd come to get Nip and Claudie. That was while she was still in high school. It had been Christmas, warm and drizzly like it always got for Christmas. The front door had opened and there Sonny was, wearing that ridiculous overcoat that seemed to weigh him down. That overcoat of expensive British tweed with a belt in the back and Sonny peeping out from behind it like some sort of wild animal. He'd brought a case of whiskey that time—a whole damned case—half of which she had managed at one time or another to pour down the drain. Irene never knew how much had been drunk anyway. He'd stayed three days, walking the floor and looking out the windows onto the highway, wearing the overcoat half the time. And when he'd gone back Nip had been driving the long black car and Claudie had been enthroned in the back seat, her eyes shining in her black face at the thought of New England wages.

After that she and her mother had done the housework. There wasn't anybody else who would work for them for what Nip and Claudie would. Nip and Claudie were Colvin Negroes. Their great-grandfather had been freed by Great-great-grandfather Colvin just before the Civil War. But sonny wanted Nip and Claudie. And Nip and Claudie wanted the North.

Laura Lee scrubbed fiercely at her face with the tepid water. It was strange to her to think how much she still cared about Sonny. By all reason she shouldn't like him at all. But, she thought with self-scorn, I'm as bad as Mama. I still think of him as the white hope of the Colvins. I'm still enthralled by the old charm. All of us, sitting here in the rot, waiting for Sonny. And Sonny couldn't care less. Her mother said he had come back again once while she was at college, bringing Nip and Claudie with him, both of them all diked out in fancy clothes. But that visit hadn't turned out too well either. He hadn't been back since.

She got out of the tub and began to dress, putting on an old pair of gloves to put on her hose, rubbing carefully at a small spot on her white shoes. Her neatness was one of the things Carter liked best about her and she never let him know the pains it took to maintain it; the hours washing over the low sink, ironing on the old legless ironing board propped across two kitchen chairs, the endless shoe polishing and underwear rinsing, heating water to wash her hair twice a week. All of it when she was so tired, so damned tired of that office and the people in it and the endless smell of the unwashed who traipsed through it.

She rubbed lotion on her hands, looking at the small moonstone ring on her right hand. Sonny had brought her that the Christmas he'd come home. That and a black velveteen dress. Irene had taken the dress because she said it was too old for her.

She could hear the sound of cabinet doors being opened and slammed shut downstairs and she tensed, listening toward the sound. Then the front door slammed and she could hear her mother's voice raised and her father's answering in his soft mumble.

She fixed her face and hair quickly. In a few moments she heard footsteps on the stairs. Her mother came into the room. "Laura," she said, looking over her head. "Do you have any money?"

"No."

"Just a couple of bucks . . ."

"No. I spent what I had extra on the plumber this week. You know that."

"I thought maybe . . ."

"No."

"When Carter comes . . ."

"You aren't going to see Carter," Laura Lee said slowly. "He never comes in."

"I thought you might borrow . . ."

"No, Mama," Laura Lee said. "I'm not going to borrow *anything* from Carter."

"Laura Lee," Irene said, her voice changing. "What makes you so funny?"

"I can't imagine," Laura Lee said. "There's sure nothing funny about anybody else in this family." She gathered up her purse and walked out of the room.

Her father still sat in his rocker looking out into the darkness. She sat in the swing again. "Hello, honey," J.O. said. "You smell mighty good."

"Just soap, Papa." She looked toward the street. "What're you watching?" she said.

"Night. Just the night."

"It's nice, isn't it, night? I've gotten to where I like it a lot better than daytime. Maybe that's because of the job. Maybe . . . Oh, I don't know, but it's better than daylight to me now."

"It hides things," J.O. said. "There's no doubt of that."

The McCain house stood alone on a narrow dirt road that ran behind Graves' Sawmill. It was a white frame

28

building, originally of four rooms but with a new concrete block addition and a new carport. Around it the woods grew into the yard and behind it they still held the terrain. Carter had lived here since he was five years old. He remembered no other home.

He looked at Estelle sitting quiet beside him. "You want to run by the house and pick up some more whiskey?" he said.

"All right. I don't know what Dupree's got in the house."

He swung the car off the highway and past the sawmill, enjoying as he always did the fresh sharp smells of new-cut wood and oozing rosin. It was dark except for the small naked bulb in the kiln. He drove past and onto the road toward home. There were no cars yet; it was early.

He pulled into the yard and stopped, careful not to block the drive. He could see his mother's car under the carport and the pickup pulled up by the house.

"You want to come in?" he said.

"I guess."

They got out and walked across the bare yard. From the steps they could hear Will's voice raised in protest and the calmer tones of Mrs. McCain. Then the front door slammed and Will came out on the porch. He stood looking at them, his hands in his hip pockets. Then he leaned over and spat off the edge of the porch. "Well, now," he said, grinning. "Back so soon? How come you bringing her out here, Carter? You think Dupree's had time to get his shotgun?"

"Oh, can it, Will," Carter said. "Estelle's come as a customer."

"What'd you like, Estelle?" Will said. "Some imported champagne? A fifth of Johnnie Walker?"

Estelle looked at him. She shrugged her thin shoulders. "I don't know what I'd like," she said. "But what I'll get is a pint of Seagram's."

Will laughed. "Make Mama give you a snort of the private stock while you're in there," he said. "You look sort of peaked."

"I'll do that," Estelle said. She walked by him and into the house.

Will put a hand on Carter's arm. "Arlie's looking for you," he said. "He and Hobson are planning on some sort of doings later tonight, I take it."

"O.K.," Carter said. "I'll see him."

"You got a date with Miss Colvin?"

"It's none of your damned business," Carter said. He moved past Will and started through the door.

"Don't get huffy," Will said. "I ain't gonna hurt her none by talking about her, am I? I am willing to accept your assurance that she's cherry as all hell. I just can't figure out why you're dating her or her you, that's all."

"Don't start it again, Will," Carter said. "I date who I damn well please." He went on into the house.

The living room was a small square room, bare except for a matched suite of heavy rose brocade with tasseled edges and a vase of red paper roses on the mantel. Carter walked on through it and into the kitchen. His mother was standing by the refrigerator talking to Estelle and he knew that in a minute she was going to drag out a bottle of her own Jack Daniels and give Estelle a drink. He grinned. She never did that unless she liked the person a hell of a lot. He was right. She opened the refrigerator and brought out the bottle. "Have a touch of this," she said to Estelle. "It'll make you feel better and help you too."

Estelle smiled. She was sitting on a kitchen chair and some of the color had come back into her face. "That'd be mighty good," she said.

Bertha McCain poured a good three ounces into a jelly glass. "Go get her a pint, Carter," she said. She tucked Estelle's five-dollar bill into a cooky jar and handed her the glass.

Carter went through the breakfast room into the back room. He reached up and got a pint out of the stacked cases. He looked at it for a moment, thinking of all the people who came here for the merchandise stacked in this little room. It always had made him sad. Ever since the days when he'd first known why so many of the people of Bellefonte came to their house. All the people of Bellefonte, the poor and dirty and the well-groomed and rich. There weren't as many of them as there used to be because it wasn't too long a drive to Hunter City and the state liquor store. Everybody had a car now. But there were still enough of them; because everybody ran out. It is when the last of the fifth is gone and it is two A.M.

that five dollars for a pint doesn't seem in the least exorbitant.

He took the bottle back into the kitchen. Estelle was sitting at the table now, watching Bertha at the stove. "You haven't eaten yet, have you?" she said. "Will hadn't but he wouldn't wait for me to fix nothing. That's what we were fussing about. He never stays here long enough to eat. Especially when his daddy leaves him the pickup."

"I never did hear him drive off," Carter said.

"Maybe he's waiting after all." Bertha took the pork chops off the stove and the biscuits out of the oven. "Let's eat," she bellowed.

Will came into the house. "Well," he said belligerently. "I figured I might as well eat while I'm here."

"Daddy already gone to work?" Carter said.

Bertha nodded. "Had to take the early shift tonight," she said. Dickson McCain worked for the state. He was night watchman at the gravel pit up the highway. That was how, ostensibly, he made his money. Or at least it was the way the sheriff had worked out for him to make his money.

"You eat now, Estelle," Bertha said.

Estelle looked at the food, her mouth worked, and she jumped up and ran toward the new wing of the house.

"What's the matter with her?" Bertha said.

Carter shook his head.

"She and Carter been up to something," Will said, his mouth full of food.

"Shut up," Carter said. He ate. He wasn't hungry, but he knew he probably would be later, when he wouldn't have time to eat.

"You dressed for the night?" Will said.

"He changed his shirt this afternoon," Bertha said. "He looks clean to me."

"Well, he's got a date with the princess, so I figured maybe he'd be wearing a suit," Will said.

"What you got against that girl, Will?" Bertha said.

Will made a face. "I went to school with her," he said. "Remember? Miss Colvin, with her nose ten feet in the air. Besides I never liked that brother. Remember him?"

"What happened to that boy, anyway?" Bertha said. "He still up north?"

"Still up there and still up to no good, I'll vow," Will

31

said. He stood up and lit a cigarette. "Good night, lovely people," he said. "I'm gone." He went out the door and they could hear him starting the pickup and roaring off up the road.

Bertha shook her head. "I better go see about that girl," she said. She stood up but just then Estelle came back into the room. "You ready to go, Carter?" she said. "I want to get home."

He nodded and got up. "Let me pick up my box."

He went through the breakfast room again and out the other door to the new wing. His bedroom still smelled of new plaster and paint. It was large and airy and the first room of his own he'd ever had. There was a white iron bed, a pine chest, a straight chair. And, in the corner, his hi-fi set. He had paid a good deal of money for it, driven across a lot of miles of rough road for it, but here it was. In the cabinet next to it was his collection of records. He looked at them lovingly. He had all the original Jimmie Rodgers 78's. He'd found them in the attic of his aunt's house in Georgia. She'd been glad to get rid of them. They were in almost perfect condition. They'd belonged to a boarder in the house she kept for railroaders and she'd taken them for back rent along with his clothes. That had been back in the thirties, and until the day Carter discovered them they had lain in their manila and pasteboard albums in the back of his aunt's attic.

He took his guitar from the top of the chest and went back to the kitchen.

Estelle smiled at him. "You going serenading tonight?" she said.

"Probably."

"You sure can play that thing."

A car horn sounded outside, and they followed Bertha into the living room. There were steps in the yard and Julie and Jake came into the light on the porch.

"Well, hi," Carter said. "Come on in."

"Hiddy boy," Jake said. "What do you think of your old uncle escorting the prettiest girl in town?"

Julie smiled and patted Jake's arm. They came on into the living room. "Where's that Will?" Jake said.

"Didn't you pass him?" Carter said. "He just slammed out of here."

Jake shook his head. "The way he drives probably already to town before we started. Arlie Machen's looking for you."

"Anything special?" Carter looked at Julie.

She shrugged. "Wants to go somewhere after you meet the train tonight," she said. "I'm going back and talk to your mama a minute." She put her hand on Bertha's arm and they started through the kitchen door. Julie stopped and looked at Estelle's face. "You all right, Essie?" she said.

Estelle nodded.

"No you're not," Julie said. "I'm going back to town with you." She went on into the kitchen. "I could use a pint," she said to Bertha. "And a cup of coffee while you're getting it."

Bertha grinned. She poured the coffee into a heavy mug and handed it to Julie. "Want your money's worth?" she said. "Sit down and have a bite."

Julie shook her head. "I want to get Estelle into town," she said. "She doesn't look good."

"Sort of peaked," Bertha said. "Been drinking, I think. What's she doing with Carter anyway?"

Julie shook her head. "Doing something for Dupree," she said. She set her empty cup on the table. "Want me to get the whiskey?" she said.

"You know where it is?"

"Watched you get it enough." She walked over to the storeroom and got a pint of whiskey, opened her purse and put the five dollars on the table. "See, that's what you get when you take on steady customers."

Bertha laughed. "Hell, I don't reckon there's anybody in Maynard County don't know where it is," she said.

"We're going," Carter said from the next room.

"All right." Julie opened her purse and put the bottle in it. She smiled at Bertha. "Hold 'em down," she said, going out.

"You going back in with us, Uncle Jake?" Carter said.

"Think I'll stick around and talk to Bertha a while," he said. "Ride in with somebody coming out later."

Julie and Carter walked onto the wooden porch. Estelle was already sitting in the taxi, her head back against the seat. "You want me to take her with me?" Julie said. "I got Arlie's car."

Carter shook his head. "I promised Dupree to get her

33

home. I'll take her. If I don't see Arlie, tell him it's O.K. about tonight."

"All right. You bringing Laura Lee?"

"I reckon."

Julie smiled. "She's pretty," she said.

Carter got into his car and slammed the door. "Thanks," he said.

Arlie Machen sat in a cane-bottomed straight chair tilted back against the white cement wall of his gas station. From where he sat he could see most of the town of Bellefonte. He could see down the east side of the square and up the north side and across the square itself to the courthouse and the parking spaces around it. Looking north he could see the newspaper office and the post office, looking south he could see Jackson Ferguson walking up the block toward him. He lit a cigarette and snapped the match onto the cement. A car drove up and he motioned the boy helping him to wait on it. It had an out-of-county tag and he watched the occupants idly —college boys from Hunter City probably dating some local girls.

Will McCain pulled in behind the car, a new Rambler, and got out of his pickup, slamming the door. He looked disgustedly at the occupants of the car and came over to Arlie. "Couple of college hots chasing the local tail," he said. He sat down in another chair and tilted back beside Arlie. "Oh, well. Little business for the folks maybe."

"Seen Carter?" Arlie said.

"He's out at the house with that Estelle and Julie," Will said. "Must be getting tired of Miss Goody-goody."

Arlie shook his head. "You know damned well Carter ain't having nothing to do with Dupree's wife. Why do you aways talk like that?"

Will shrugged. "She looks ready to me," he said.

"You ain't Carter," Arlie said. He stood up and stretched. Jackson Ferguson had reached the corner and was waiting for the light before crossing to their corner of the square. He stood with his hand on his blackjack, watching the parked cars. Arlie threw his cigarette down and stepped on it. He watched while Jackson crossed toward them, his eyes sweeping the gas station, and stopped to wait for the light before crossing again to the

34

north side of the square. Arlie turned his back on him and sat down again.

The printer passed by and went on down the street, turning into the newspaper office. Two girls walked by toward the post office. Arlie watched them incuriously until they were out of sight. The Rambler pulled out and Julie drove in and parked Arlie's car at the side of the station. She got out and brought the keys over to him. She glanced at Will. He grinned and she turned her back on him and spoke to Arlie. "It's hot as hell tonight," she said. "You can still see the tar melting on the streets."

"Good loving weather," Arlie said out of the corner of his mouth. "Sweat . . ."

"Oh hush," Julie said, smiling at him. "Saw Carter. He says it's O.K. for tonight. He's bringing Laura Lee . . . and the guitar."

"Fine," Arlie said. "Where you heading?"

"Back down to the café," she said. "Thought I'd hang around with Estelle awhile."

"All right." Arlie stood up again. "Come back down later," he said. "I'll know better what time I can get away."

"All right." She put her hand out and touched him lightly on the sleeve. Then she walked off quickly, her high heels clicking on the cement.

"That's a good-looking gal," Will said. "What's she doing here anyway?"

"None of my business," Arlie said.

"Don't you wonder?" Will said. "Ain't you got any natural curiosity? She don't work, she don't belong to nobody. She's got to have some kind of reason for being here."

"Maybe she likes it," Arlie said.

Will laughed. "Picked it off the map with a pin maybe," he said. "But why would anybody do that? Where's she from?"

"Virginia somewhere, I think," Arlie said.

"Don't talk like it."

"She's been away from there a long time."

He wished Will would shut up because he didn't want to talk about what bothered him too. He'd thought about all the reasons why Julie could be in Bellefonte and he didn't like the answers he got. He could have asked her point-blank; but he never had. He knew that he didn't want to know.

He had always been that way. Because usually the answers to the questions you asked turned out to be bad. It was better to delay it as long as possible.

He had been seven years old before he asked the question that had worried him for all the time he could remember. They lived in a neat brown house outside of town, his mother, his grandmother and grandfather, and him. They had a cow and chickens and a hog, and they grew cotton and one field of corn and the silage for the cow. When he was six he went to school on the big yellow bus with his cousins. He had a lot of cousins because his mother had four brothers. The Machens were a big sprawling family that together owned a good strip of land. But he didn't have any brothers and sisters and he didn't have any daddy. That was the question he had harbored for most of his life. Where was his daddy? He asked his mother one July day when they'd gone off to his uncle Mat's to an all-day reunion.

The kids all went down to the creek to swim and wait for the ice cream. "My daddy's going to buy some new land closer in to town," Billy Fred had said. Billy Fred was his oldest cousin, a big strong boy with a freckled face and straight white hair. "It's a shame you ain't got no daddy to get you moved in closer to school."

"I got a daddy," Arlie said. "Grandfather's my daddy."

Billy Fred shook his head. He was sitting on the creek-bank in a pair of cut-off jeans, still wet with creek water. The other kids sprawled around him, and some of the girls giggled.

"Grandfather's all our grandfather," Bill Fred said importantly. "You have to have a daddy too and you ain't got one."

"Oh, everybody has one," Mary Emma said. She was his favorite cousin, even though she was a girl. "He's just not here, that's all."

"No," Billy Fred said importantly. "He don't have one at all. That's why he's named Machen just like all the rest of us even though that's his mama's name."

Arlie looked at him. There wasn't anything to say because it was true. It was hot in the tangled undergrowth around the creek, hot and muggy and sticky. He could

36

feel his skin, damp and prickly and stinging where bits of grass stuck to him. It was very quiet. All the kids had stopped laughing and talking and were watching him. He didn't want to fight Billy Fred, he knew he had no chance of winning against him, but he thought maybe he ought to try. He had put one puny fist up when Billy Fred laughed. He said, "I ain't gonna fight a runt like you, Arlie. You just ask your mama about it. You do that." Then he had run and dived off into the creek.

Arlie stood watching the ripples where he'd gone in, knowing he ought to jump after him and knowing too that he didn't swim that well. He had no chance of getting in one lick in the water. Mary Emma put her hand on his arm. "Don't pay him any attention," she said. "He just likes to be the top dog with all of us."

Arlie shook her off and ran out of the clearing. He got tangled in a briar patch on the way back to the picnic ground and by the time he reached his mother, who was standing over the picnic table ladling peach pickle out of the big brown crock, he was bleeding and dirty and crying.

She put the ladle down and came toward him. "Why, Arlie baby," she said. "What on earth happened?"

He pulled back, looking hard at her. He thought his mother was very beautiful. She was tall and big and brown-faced, with black hair pulled back behind her ears, but now he didn't want her to touch him. "Where's my daddy?" he said, trying hard to stop crying. "Where is my daddy?"

She looked at him and put her hand to her hair and pushed at it. "Arlie," she said. "Your daddy doesn't live with us. He . . ." She stopped, the words she had rehearsed in the back of her mind for seven years failing her now. "He didn't want to live with us," she said.

She had lived all her life on the farm of her father. She liked it. Others of her family, the brothers, their wives, longed for town. She never had. She liked the rowed dirt outside the kitchen window, the morning sunlight on the bare wood floors, the smell of earth and hay and barnyard. Only that once had she ever wanted anything more.

She had been sixteen and it was spring. March in Alabama. There were jonquils growing cool and yellow and green out of black ground. There were redbud trees, blooming a muted scarlet in the still chill air. At night the sun-warmed days cooled back toward winter. At midday it was as hot as July. She had met him at the first picnic at Sinkler's Mill. He was a stranger, come to spend a few days helping out with the plowing at Otis Matthews'. She had seen him, standing silent and scowling by a picnic table, watching the others laughing, running, eating in the sunlit afternoon. She had loved him and wanted him in that moment as simply and completely as the growing life around her. She watched him steadily until he noticed her.

The next day he walked her home from church. The next night they went together to the edge of the creek and in darkness and burgeoning spring made love on the ground still damp with winter cold.

She met him every night for the two weeks of his stay, and she would have followed him anywhere, but he left without her, without even telling her good-by. Unless the last night, the last dark restless mating, could have said that.

When she knew she was pregnant she sent for him through Otis Matthew's oldest daughter. He came, walking quietly up through the back field and standing just beyond the kitchen garden. She went out to him. "I'm going to have a baby," she said.

She felt then that he looked at her, really looked for the first time. "I hadn't counted on that," he said.

"It's what happens," she'd said.

"I hadn't counted on it," he said again.

"I love you," she said then, throwing pride behind her. "I'll do whatever you want. We'll go away from here, or you can come and work for Pa. It don't matter. We'll do whatever you want."

He shook his head, looking at her, his eyes somber and without thought for her in them. "I don't know," he said, disposing of her sacrifice of home in three words. "I ain't too good a hand with crops."

"You don't want me," she said.

He looked at her again, letting recognition into his face. "That ain't it either," he said. "I just didn't count on it."

It had been terrible then, and to think of it now after seven years was still terrible to her. It was the simple fact of his indifference, that solid calm indifference planted against the love and longing and bursting sweetness inside her. She couldn't fight it, nor did she want to. "I'll just have to make out the best I can then," she'd said.

"I'm sorry," he said. "I'm real sorry this had to happen."

"Get on out of here," she said, mad by now, hating him momentarily by now, wanting somehow someway to take back all the love and giving, and knowing she was trapped with it for the rest of her life. "Get out of here before I go tell my brothers."

He turned and went.

She remembered now too, looking at Arlie, all that frantic spring and summer with her brothers dashing around the countryside like a company of madmen, looking for somebody they didn't even know. Because she never told them. He hadn't wanted her, or Arlie. And she had no desire to have him forced to accept them. It was true enough he hadn't wanted to live with them. But she hadn't wanted him either, not after knowing how badly he wanted to get away.

"He didn't want to live with us," she said again.

"Then I *have* got a daddy," Arlie said.

"Yes. Yes. Everybody has a daddy," she said slowly, watching him, seeing in his eyes the blank intractable self-center that had gazed at her across the garden patch those years ago, seeing in him the thing that tied her forever to the past and to the present he made himself, love. Love, given for no reason, and the only answer to it being, I hadn't counted on that. She hadn't counted on this from Arlie either. It was the sad lost way of the world. She put a hand out toward him but he took another step backward. "Where is he?" he said.

"Arlie . . ."

"Where is he, Mama?"

She hadn't wanted to lie to him, but she did then, saying the only thing she knew to say, the only thing that came handy after seven years of wondering what that thing would be. "He's away from here, a long way away. He's out in Texas."

"What's his name?" Arlie said.

She stared at the small implacable figure, seeing in him the face and nature of the only man she had ever loved or hated. "It doesn't matter, Arlie," she said. "You have your grandmother and granddaddy, and your mama. We all love you very much. It doesn't matter. You'll see that when you're older."

He took another step away and put his hand up to his face to wipe at a trickle of blood from one of the briar scratches. "It's true then," he said. "I ain't got no daddy. If I did have you'd know his name and it'd be my name. Billy Fred's right."

"Arlie!" She started toward him, but he turned and ran out of the picnic grounds and back toward the road. He ran a long time until the sun made him stop under a roadside tree. He rested only a minute, then ran on. When he got home he went straight to his room and crawled under the bed where it was dark and cool. When his mother's voice called to him he didn't answer her.

"What the hell you thinking about, Arlie?" Will said. "They's a guy trying to get your attention over yonder."

Arlie looked up. There were two cars by the tanks now and the boy was having trouble handling both of them. He walked over and went to work on the second car. The night was dark now, the way he liked it. Most of the buildings around him were dark too with only the bright neon splashes in front of the drugstores and cafés, the small wavering beacon of the newspaper office, and the blue ghostliness of the street lamps. He took the credit card from the driver and went into the station with it. It was very clean inside the building with the tires and tubes and cans stacked neatly on freshly painted racks. He went back out. When the car drove off he went to the corner and looked down the street toward the taxi ranks a block off the square. He didn't see Carter's car among the lighted cabs and he went back to his chair against the wall.

"You ain't much company tonight," Will said.

Arlie shrugged, and Will got up and walked toward the corner. "Might as well try to stir something up," he said.

"See you," Arlie said. He lit another cigarette. He knew who his father was now. He'd found that out a long time ago. But it hadn't changed anything. By that time he had given up the daylight, ceased to like it or want to be abroad in it. He'd finished high school because of his mother. After that he drove a truck for a couple of years. He drove explosives because that was where the money was and now he had the station and the place on the

40

square where he could sit at night and watch the other side of day. He liked it.

Jackson Ferguson stood for a long time in front of the Majestic Café after his last cup of coffee. He had a good view here of the busiest part of the square. He could see the front of both drugstores and both motion-picture houses, and he commanded a close view of the entrance to the café. It was in these places he always expected to see the beginnings, the vague rumblings of trouble.

He watched the Hobson girl come up the block from the filling station and he let his mind wonder on her again. He had seen her somewhere before she came to Bellefonte. He was sure of it. At first it had been only a vague nagging at the back of his mind, Who did she look like? Now it had become an insistent small question, Where had he seen her? He wasn't mistaken. He didn't make that kind of mistake. He couldn't afford to. Now that he was getting older he watched faces more closely, he learned walks, he memorized gestures. They would never put him off the force for a case of false arrest. There were those who were after him. He knew that too. You couldn't enforce the law without making enemies. And nowadays with the college graduates trying to run the city government the small-minded do-gooders were acquiring too much influence. They wanted the law enforced but they didn't want anybody enforcing it. That was how they talked anyway. So he was careful. He'd been careful for the five years since the incident with that Colvin nigger. He'd seen Julie Hobson before.

She walked by him and went into the café, not even glancing toward him. He watched her through the window, going in and sitting down at the counter. There was something unpleasant about the time he'd seen her, too, but he couldn't get hold of that either. He would, though. He knew it was there somewhere in the back of his mind and that in time he was going to bring it up. He just had to wait.

He watched over Bellefonte, noting the parked cars, the street idlers, the drugstore bunch. Later he would go off the square and look over the filling stations and the taxi stand and the poolroom. It wasn't really late enough for that yet.

41

He had watched over this town for a long time now, for so long that he had forgotten the kind of life lived in daylight. Sometimes, getting up in the cramped apartment in the old house owned by his wife's parents, something about the slant of the sun would make him hungry for morning. But it never lasted long. He had had enough of the sun back on his father's farm in the adjoining county. He never really regretted the loss of it.

His wife lived in the daytime. She had never adapted her life to his. He didn't care, she didn't interest him any more. She had been a pale, fairly pretty girl once, a long time ago. Now she was only the short fat woman who cooked his meals and spent her evenings in the picture show, her daylight hours in some way unfathomable to him. They had no children. He had ceased caring about that too now. It was the young ones who lived with trouble. He was just as glad not to have that worry. He knew that his wife was afraid of him. He had known that for a long time too, and it suited him now to let her be. It ensured him three indifferently cooked meals a day and the clean sheets he insisted on every morning. It kept her out of his way. He had never given her reason to fear him. He had never threatened nor struck her, nor even raised his voice to her in all the years they'd lived together. But he had never let her know him either. He often wondered why she didn't go away.

A car pulled to the curb in front of the café. He watched the occupants, the oldest McCain boy and Dupree Harris' wife. They got out and went past him. "Evening, Mr. Ferguson," Carter said.

He nodded. Estelle didn't look at him. She opened the door of the café before Carter could reach it and went inside. Ferguson ignored Carter. He'd been warned about the McCains the time he'd spoken to Will about scuffling in the poolroom. For all he cared he could be bringing whiskey into the damned café to sell. He wouldn't endanger his job for a bootlegger—not unless he could really catch him up to something. He saw them sit down on either side of Julie Hobson and he frowned. They were all looking toward the front of the restaurant now and he moved away and started down North Street. He'd get hold of where he'd seen that one yet.

At the next corner he saw a crowd of boys turning toward the poolroom and he noted carefully who they were. Behind him the loudspeaker began to blare music from the picture show onto the sidewalk. He quickened his step toward the traffic light on the corner. It was already turning green.

"Why's he standing out there like that?" Estelle said nervously.

"Been hanging around all night," Dupree said. "Must have gotten a tip that something's going to happen." He watched Estelle covertly. She seemed well enough, he thought. A little pale maybe and her eyes were funny, but that could be the whiskey. She was drinking steadily from a pint in her purse. "You want me to get somebody in to help Annie and take you on home, honey?" he said.

Estelle shook her head. "I'd rather be up here." She smiled at Dupree. "I'm all right, baby. Why don't you fix us something to eat? I think I can eat now."

Dupree turned toward the grill and Estelle poured some more whiskey into her tumbler. Carter shoved his coffee cup away from him and stood up. "I got to get back down to the taxi stand," he said. "I got to where I loaf too damned much. You gonna stay with her, Julie?"

Julie nodded. "See you later," she said.

Carter looked uncertainly at Estelle and Dupree. "I'm going," he said.

Dupree came over to him. "Well, thanks, Carter," he said slowly, not looking at him. "I'll pay you up later."

Carter nodded and went out. He stood for a moment on the outside of the café looking in at them. They sat tiredly in the bright lights, Estelle hunched over her glass, Julie looking into her cup, Dupree working over the grill. He felt depressed suddenly, overwhelmed by the brightness of the lights and the brilliant colors of the dresses and shirts and hair oil and lipstick that covered them. It made him think of Halloween, a night that had always depressed him with its noise and color and bright orange and black masks and noisemakers and leering pumpkins. It was on Halloween that the wish to live in daylight was strongest in him. It had been on a Halloween night when he'd seen Blackjack Ferguson beat that nigger right on the street corner with all the people standing watching, even the kids in their costumes with their tambourines. Just standing there, watching, while he hit him in the

43

head and kept on hitting him and finally drug him away like a limp sack of meal.

He went on out to the street and got into his cab. At the corner he pulled over and tapped the horn at Arlie. Arlie got up and came over to the car, leaning his elbows on the window. "Hi," he said. "You want to toss a few tonight?"

"O.K.," Carter said. "I guess Laura Lee'll be with me. It's Saturday."

He drove on to the taxi stand. Will was leaning against the lighted telephone that was nailed onto the corner telephone pole. He watched Carter sardonically. "No fares tonight?" he said.

Carter parked and got out of the car. "Don't you ever do anything but loaf?" he said.

"Not to speak of." Will lit a cigarette and leaned back against the phone. "Now when I get into the para-troopers . . ." he said softly.

"Yeah," Carter said. "You're going to be a hero. I know all about it. You'd do better to think about getting through high school first."

Will shrugged and pushed himself away from the phone. "What I need," he said, "is a good woman to do for me. One like you got."

"Lay off," Carter said. He swung around and got back in the cab. Before switching on the lights he looked back up the street toward the square. The night lay thick now outside the small pools of light. There were few people on the street. He switched on the lights and drove off.

Early in the evening he often cruised around the town, ostensibly looking for a fare, in actuality watching the town settle into night. It had become a game with him, seeing the emergence of the night faces, the night per-sonalities. Bellefonte changed its character to match the shadow side. He had watched them for years from his seat behind the wheel, the people of the day in their night clothes, with night words on their lips and nighttime actions, actions brought out only nocturnally, words and actions that found no place in the market place of day.

It gave him a peculiar view of people. Sometimes, read-ing items in the local paper, he would laugh, able to see on the printed page the day images of people he knew to be someone else. There was Mrs. Butler. On the pages of the *Maynard County Mast* she spent vacations in Europe,

44

she entertained at teas, and contributed to charities. Carter McCain knew Mrs. Butler as a dark figure who furtively carried all her empty whiskey bottles down the hill from her fenced brick house and deposited them carefully in the garbage cans belonging to her nearest neighbor, the wife of a local banker. It was Mrs. Butler's contention that everybody *knew* the banker's wife drank, and a few more bottles couldn't hurt her. There was Carolyn Tate who in the sunlit afternoons sat on the edge of the pool at the country club, entertaining out-of-town guests. At night she walked two snarling pekinese down the street by the Methodist church, and at ten-thirty on Wednesday and Friday evenings she got into the car belonging to the owner of a local store.

There were all the people who came to his father's house: the gay, the furtive, the driven, clutching their five-dollar bills in sweated hands. And there were all the girls. The laughing healthy dreaming girls of day, who with night became the painted temptress, the perfumed image of desire, the comforting motherwarmth of dark.

They were all sojourners in his world. They came into it at twilight and were gone from it before dawn. Except for Laura Lee, who tried to live in both worlds. Laura Lee, and the others like her, running from day to night and back again. And those others, the ones like Laura Lee's mother, Irene Colvin, those who belonged to night and tried to pretend they didn't. He'd seen Irene Colvin in the night too, at times and places he would never tell Laura Lee about.

He thought sadly of Estelle and the tired dirty feeling the trip with her had given him. That small neat house in Longstreet, Georgia, belonged to night, a place where the mistakes made in darkness could be eradicated in darkness. And it wasn't even horrible. Only dingy and furtive and dirty in an ordinary way.

He drove steadily through the darkened streets, watching for something. The truth was that he was afraid. The fear came to him periodically. It had since before he could remember the attendant circumstances. It was a sudden tightening of muscle, a defensive defiant gesture, tuned and turned toward something he didn't understand. Because he felt what the fear really was, knew that if he turned and faced it solidly he could name it, maybe even

45

own it and conquer it. But he wouldn't. Because just as certainly the fear might win. It was fear all right, but not of any external thing. The thing he feared lived in himself, showing claws sometimes, but never revealing itself. It was a dark and dwelling mass within him, pushed back by talk and music and girls and food and drink. And it was like the night, dark and undefined and full of anticipation. He lived with it, waiting for the time when the thing, whatever it was, would try the bars and with his help escape. Because he knew that too. Only he could let it out, and when the time came he would. He'd do it consciously and with a sort of dark joy. He knew that much about himself. He'd known it forever. It was the real reason he didn't escape to the streets of day.

Once when he had been much younger, nineteen to Will's twelve, on a summer night, like tonight, hot and dark and dreaming, they had come up the road from the river toward home, holding their cane poles in their hands, laughing together, feeling the sunburn across their noses, wanting supper and the comfort of lights and home. Will had stopped on the dirt road, listening into the darkness, seeming to hear more than the sound of tree frogs in the early night. "There's somebody out there," he'd said. He motioned toward the trees on the roadside.

"So what?" Carter had said. "There's always somebody out there. It's a pretty place for it."

"I want to see it," Will said.

"No."

Will had laughed softly, coming closer to him to peer into his face. Then he had whispered to him, the sound hot and sticky as the breath in his face. "That's just like you, Carter," Will said, sounding then, already at twelve years old, older than Carter felt himself. "You want it and you like it and I know damned well you do it—with Lacey Jones for one." He laughed again, the sound unnerving to Carter in the darkness. "But you want it in the dark, don't you, Carter? You couldn't take it in daylight, or moonlight, or starlight. You're an under-the-cover man, aren't you?"

Carter had stood there, the fear rising up in him like the evening breeze from the river, watching while Will laid down his cane fishing pole and ducked under the barbed-wire fence and disappeared into the trees beside the road.

Around him there had been tree frogs and stars and dust and night. And in him only blackness. He went home, hating himself and Will and the dark and the sound of female laughter. But with all of it wanting a woman so badly he'd gone out after supper and taken Lacey Jones into her father's cotton house. And done it in the dark, he told himself. Don't forget that. You did it in the dark and that made it better. He cursed bitterly in the silence of the car.

He saw a figure on the corner of College Street and swerved suddenly to the curb. It was Charlene Webster, a girl he'd known in high school. She was dressed in black, with a rhinestone necklace and high-heeled shoes. "Want a taxi, Charlene?" he said.

"Yes, I do," she said. "I started up to Sue Benson's house and these damned shoes are killing me." She came around and got into the front seat with him. He could smell her perfume and underneath it the clean smell of soap. She was very young and pretty and the expectant quality hung over her like a mist.

"Party?" he said.

"Uh-huh. It's Sue's birthday. All the girls are going early because it's a spend-the-night, and Daddy went off somewhere in the car, so here I am, walking around like an idiot in these heels."

He drove her to the Bensons' without speaking again. She had become part of his restlessness. He remembered her in a sweater and skirt in chemistry lab, and in worn blue jeans on the class picnic. He saw her now translated into night. He was afraid she might touch him. He knew that if she did he would hate her suddenly, and for no cause. He stopped the car.

"Fifty cents?" she said.

He nodded and she fumbled in a little black purse and gave him a dollar bill. He made the change.

"Do you still play the guitar, Carter?" she said.

He nodded. "Some."

"You were awfully good."

"Thanks," he said. "Have a good time."

"Sure." She got out of the cab quickly and went up the concrete walk, her heels making small bright taps in the darkness. He watched her as the door opened and she

47

walked into light. "I need Laura Lee," he thought. "I might as well get her and let her ride with me."

He drove to the house on the highway in a sudden hurry.

She was sitting on the porch. He could see the gleam of her white dress from the curb. He parked and tapped the horn. She came down the steps quickly, waving her hand to someone behind her on the porch, and got into the car. He drove for a block before he looked at her. "Hi," he said.

She moved toward him and touched his cheek briefly with hers.

"You smell good," he said. "Like soap."

She laughed, her voice low and warm. "You're early," she said. "You taking me with you tonight?"

"I thought I might."

She stretched, her one provocative gesture. She did it invariably when she first got in the car, and it always had the same effect on him. He parked at the curb and took her in his arms. She came quickly toward him as she always did, warm, eager, but with a sort of innate innocence that frightened him. He felt that if he did take her, suddenly one night, she would submit to that too with the same innate innocence and he would be shut out forever. He couldn't explain the feeling, but he knew it to be true. For this reason he had never really tried to take her. He pretended he wanted to, of course, for himself as well as for her, but he knew that he would never really push it to a conclusive act or commitment. They existed in an adolescent, high-school merging of lips and hands and breath. It was the sort of affair he knew himself to have outgrown, but one which he knew he liked and yearned for with Laura Lee. It was a going back to something he had thought gone forever. It was the one streak of daylight in his nights.

"What kind of day you had?" he said to her.

"Like always. Hot, dull."

He smiled at her. "You look cool. You look interesting."

She laughed. "You're not going to pick up any fares here," she said.

"I know." He started the car and drove to the square. There were more people on the street now, boys in groups

48

around the picture shows and drugstores, the last of the day's shoppers carrying sleepy children, the first of the night's seekers. Suppertime was past. Jackson Ferguson stood on the corner watching the cars as they passed the intersection.

"I wonder if they'll ever get him out of here," Laura Lee said.

Carter shook his head. "Not unless the control in the sheriff's office changes hands, and I don't see any signs of that. Daddy says it's not likely to change any time soon. Not next election anyway."

"You know Sonny nearly got rid of him after that trouble about Nip," Laura said.

"You know why he couldn't." It wasn't a question.

"Yes," Laura said. "Sonny's a Northerner to Bellefonte now. And I bet he'll always be a Southerner up there where he is. It must be a funny sort of feeling."

"You think a hell of a lot of your brother, don't you?" Carter stopped the car near the picture show and scanned the front of the theater.

"I guess," Laura said. "Yes. Yes, I do. Certainly more than anybody else in the family."

A heavy man detached himself from the crowd and came toward the street. "That cab being used, boy?"

"No. Come on," Carter said.

The man got in the back seat, looking at Laura Lee.

"Where to?" Carter said.

"Out to McCain's," the man said. He slumped back against the seat, breathing heavily.

At the house Carter turned around and addressed the man in the back seat. "You want me to get it?" he said.

"Yeah." The man took out his billfold and handed Carter five one-dollar bills.

"Come on, honey," Carter said. He took Laura's hand and led her onto the porch. She came with him silently. She had been here before but she always felt a stranger. They went into the kitchen. Jake and Bertha still sat at the kitchen table, drinking coffee and whiskey.

Bertha got up. "Well, hello, Laura," she said pleasantly. "Didn't expect you. Sit down and have some coffee."

"Got a fare and a customer," Carter said. He put the money on the table and got the bottle.

"You ought not take her around with you on Saturday nights," Bertha said.

"She's all right. I keep her with me."

Bertha shook her head. "Why don't you stay out here with me and Jake till he's ready to meet the train?" she said.

Laura Lee shook her head. "Thank you," she said. "He takes good care of me."

Jake was watching her silently. "Want a drink?" he said. She shook her head again.

"Where's your brother nowdays?" Jake said.

"In Rhode Island," Laura said. "He lives there now."

Jake nodded. "You've turned out real pretty," he said. "Look some like your mama used to."

Carter saw Laura Lee stiffen. For a moment he'd thought she was going to be friendly to Jake, but the moment passed. "Thanks," she said shortly.

"We'll see you," Carter said. They went back to the car.

Jake and Bertha sat looking after them. "She's a real nice girl," Bertha said. "No matter about her mama. She's real nice."

Jake shook his head. "Something's wrong about it," he said.

"What are you talking about?"

"Something about her and Carter. I don't know. Can't tell what I mean. He's too gentle with her."

"She's a nice girl," Bertha said firmly. "Have a drink."

"That ain't what I mean," Jake said. "It hadn't got nothing to do with that part of it. It's something about her he sees wrong. Like he looked at the negative of her instead of the print."

"Jake, don't start that kind of talking. I can't follow you."

Jake drank from his glass. "That was pretty good, wasn't it?" he said contentedly.

Julie Hobson still sat at the counter in the Majestic Café. She spent a good part of every night here, watching. Her first night in Bellefonte she had spent looking over the town. She had walked around the square, she had drunk coffee in each drugstore and café. Within two hours she knew the one she wanted to give her business. Dupree was the most likable of the proprietors, and the most close-mouthed. He was interested only in his wife. New people could come to Bellefonte out of the north, south, east, or west; it didn't matter to him. He served his coffee impartially across the plastic-topped counter. He never asked questions and his good will was like an aura. Estelle was different; she was all interest, all questions. But it was an interest only in Estelle. She wanted to know of other places, other people, other nights, of a life different and more exciting than her own. This Julie could supply for her without once speaking of herself.

The couple Julie lived with asked no questions. Her board had been arranged for her before she arrived and they weren't interested in her except as the representative of a little extra money for the garden, which was their only interest. Her room was small and clean, with an outside door. There were no neighbors within five hundred yards, and the nearest of them were Negroes, who never asked questions.

Arlie had been her one indulgence in Bellefonte. She didn't know how she had let it happen. It was a sort of involvement she tried to keep herself from, *had* kept herself from for most of her life. She was in love with him. She knew it was a love with only one possible end, but she let herself love him anyway. She was thirty-five years old and this one summer out of time she was going to allow herself that one indulgence.

She had started talking to him in the Majestic, where he came to eat supper. She liked the look of him, a certain graceful strength that she had always before connected with cruelty. But there was no cruelty in Arlie. It was as though, knowing the strength in himself, the capacity for cruelty, he had overcome it. It was this willed gentleness in him that began it. She wanted to know how deep it went; how much, if any, of the cruelty remained. If any of it remained, she never found it. Going to bed with him had been dark, and violent, and complete, but there was no cruelty there. So that she knew the will went deeper than consciousness, and she loved him. She had thought to pass the time, here in this small and timeless town, and time had caught her, trapped her in a hope of a never-ending summer. It was August now and the days and nights chased each other quickly through the dog days.

Not even Blackjack Ferguson with his walk around the nighttime perimeter would stop them.

There was one person in Bellefonte whom Julie had seen before she arrived here. Ferguson. She knew him, recognized him, and for the first days she had waited with a quiet fear that he would know her too. It wasn't likely. It had been a long time and he had had only a glimpse of her, but it was something they had overlooked. She saw that he watched her, but she knew he hadn't placed her yet. Even if he did, there was no real danger. But she didn't like it. He was capable of anything. She saw that in him.

Sitting here by Estelle she knew that Arlie was not her only involvement in this town. She had become more involved each night with more people. She hadn't wanted any of it to happen. She had been many places, for short times and long, she had lived among many and varied people and they had never before touched her, demanded of her, made her think of them beyond the time when she'd have to go on. Here she had been made vulnerable, perhaps by love for Arlie. They were all real to her. Dupree with his hopeless, senseless love for Estelle, Estelle herself with her hopeless longing for brighter lights, Carter McCain with his hopeless searching for daylight. Laura Lee. She stubbed out her cigarette. "How you feeling, honey?" she said to Estelle.

"I'm perfectly fine," Estelle said. "There isn't anything wrong with me. Little tight, maybe."

"Come off it, honey," Julie said. "I know. And you better be glad I do because you might be glad to have me around a little later on."

Estelle drew back from her. "Did Carter tell you?"

Julie shook her head. "You know him better than that. I can see, that's all. I wasn't born yesterday, nor in Bellefonte."

Estelle relaxed again. "Is it going to hurt bad?" she said.

"Maybe."

"For long?"

"No."

"Are you going to stay with me, Julie? I don't want Dupree to . . ."

"I'm going to stay with you," Julie said tiredly. "I promise."

"I'm scared."

"You should have been scared before you did it," Julie said calmly. "It's too late now. You'll be all right."

Jackson Ferguson came into the café for his coffee. Julie turned her back on him and went on talking to Estelle. "You want to stay up here a while longer?" she said.

Estelle nodded.

"O.K. I'll get you home when I think it's time. Arlie'll take us."

Estelle tried to smile. "You like Arlie a lot, don't you?" she said.

"Sure."

"He likes you too," Estelle said. "Dupree says he's more like a person since you've been here. Arlie's funny. Always quiet."

"I know."

"You know what he used to do?" Estelle said. "He drove explosives. Used to make me nervous just to hear about it. Imagine being up in one of those trucks out on that highway at night with all that stuff just sitting behind you. But it's just like Arlie. You'd have thought he was carting baby food. He'd come in here before a trip. Nothing at all."

"Yeah."

"Julie? You mad or something?"

"No, kid." Julie smiled. "Aren't you going to eat that steak?"

"I'll try."

Once in the dark of the tiny upstairs apartment above the garage, lying on the bed watching the rising cigarette smoke in the light from the bathroom door, Arlie had told her a story about those days of explosives. When he did talk it would be like that, suddenly, speaking out of the darkness, making a story of something, objectifying personal experience as though it were something he had read:

"Coming out of Druid City once, carrying a load of TNT, it was getting dark. That time that's in between the day and night when the road looks like it's got smoke on it and the trees are green along the side of the highway and you can see them better than you can see the lines and signs. You want to switch on the lights but something inside says, Not yet. It'll make it worse. So you wait. I hit

53

a bridge, one of those little gully crossings where it says Narrow Bridge, and two cars shouldn't ever try to pass on it. The bridge was at the foot of a dip so that you came on it blind from the back. And right there the motor went. It just quit on me for no reason, there on that goddamned bridge. It was like I'd be there forever with no daylight and no night and something coming over the hill any time now, blind onto that bridge. I got out. There was nothing to do but set flares and pray. I had to set 'em awful careful because my hands were shaking. Been driving the stuff for more than a year then, but my hands were shaking. It was like dreaming and trying to wake up. I had the flares out and the match ready when the car came over that blind hill. It was a blue Ford, brand new. There was one of those college kids driving it, at about sixty-five, not fast, but it was a blind hill. He couldn't stop and I knew it and he knew it. I just stood there, holding the dead flares in my hand and watching him come on. I could have jumped or run, but not far enough. And it was my truck and my TNT setting on that bridge. He had two choices. He could come on and try to squeeze by me and pray. Or he could go off the embankment on the other side and pray. He came on by. He didn't have two inches and he had no way of knowing he was going to have that. If I hadn't been flat on the curb he wouldn't have had it. I saw them when they went by me. There were five of them in the car, the kid driving, a blonde in the front seat with him, two girls and a boy in the back. They went by me at sixty-five an hour but I can tell you today what every one of them looked like and what they had on and the expressions they had on their faces. After they were gone I set the flares and patched up the truck and drove on into Newcastle. I drove the stuff for another year after that."

"Draw me another cup of joe, Dupree," Julie said.

Will McCain came in and sat down by her. "Anything doing around here?" he said.

"Nothing."

"I need me a girl," Will said. "What do you think about that, Essie?" He leaned around Julie and grinned at Estelle.

"I think you've come to the wrong place," Estelle said.

"Saw Carter and the princess while ago," Will said.

"Driving some ole drunk out to the place. You'd think he'd take better care of his merchandise than that."

"What's the matter with you anyway, Will?" Julie said. "You got the hots for little Laura yourself?"

Will flushed and got up from the counter. "Hell," he said. "What would I want with a snooty piece like that?"

"The usual thing," Julie said placidly.

"You're the damnedest woman I ever saw," Will said.

Julie smiled. "I think that's what you do need, come to think of it," she said. "Don't you have a girl?"

"I don't believe in no steady stuff!"

"I didn't say steady. I meant at all. Now and then. Saturday night."

"You bitch," Will said. He walked over to the jukebox and punched a quarter's worth of hillbilly selections. Then he sat down in a booth and gazed morosely out into the street. She was right, he did need it. But how the hell are you going to get it? If he had a paratrooper's uniform now . . . He dreamed, watching the splash of neon on the walk.

Carter had had half a dozen fares in the last hour, most of them whiskey customers, which added up because they always tipped him for that. Ten per cent went to Herbert Winston for maintaining the phone on the corner, the rest was his. They worked their own cabs in Bellefonte, with Herbert maintaining the stand. It paid off for everybody. He looked at Laura Lee. She sat beside him, pale and quiet. "Let's go park awhile," he said.

She nodded and he drove to the river. Here below the bridge that spanned the deepest part of the channel a dirt road led onto the docks. It was quiet here, even on Saturday night. Above them on the highway cars passed, their headlights spots of light sweeping above and away. Below them the river ran slow and sure in the dark. He kissed her for a long time, his eyes open to watch the way hers stayed closed with a frown between them as though she were in pain. He kissed her until he ached from it. Then he let her go and lit a cigarette and handed it to her before lighting one for himself.

"Do you love me?" she said.

"I'm nuts about you."

"That wasn't what I asked you." She didn't look at him, gazing out toward the river.

"Sure. I do, I guess," he said. "Yeah."

"I love you," she said quietly.

"I'm damned if I know why you should."

"That's silly. There're no reasons about it. I do."

He switched on the radio. "Hillbilly music is sexy to me," she said.

"I don't follow that."

"It just is. Maybe it's because it reminds me of you."

"You think I'm sexy?"

She laughed, but she still didn't look at him. "You dead or something?" she said.

He felt crowded. He never liked it when she talked to him this way. He never knew what to say to her. Because he wasn't sure whether she was laughing at him or not. She was like that. She'd be lying against him, melded with him into flesh and breath, then suddenly she'd say something sudden and jarring and shocking, and she'd laugh. It made him feel raw inside.

He had only one answer for it. He kissed her again. She shifted so that she lay across his lap. "Did you know your eyes are like a cat's?" she said softly.

He unbuttoned her dress and kissed her shoulders. She lay still and he moved her bra down and kissed her breasts. She made no sound; she never did when he loved her beyond kissing. It was the silence that stopped him. He wasn't used to silence. He wanted her to say something, make some sound, respond. She never did. There was a waiting quality in her, nothing else. He rebuttoned the dress. "Let's get back to town," he said. "I got to make another couple of bucks."

"What's the matter?"

Now he didn't look at her. "Nothing."

"That's what you always say when you stop."

"You want me to stop, don't you?" he said.

"I don't know."

"Jesus," he said.

"I don't. I can't help it."

"O.K." He started the car and drove back to the highway. "When you make up your mind, let me know," he said, trying to keep his voice light.

"Why don't you . . . Oh, hell," she said.

"Why don't I what?"

"Nothing."

"You started to say something," he said.

"It sounds silly."

"Say it."

"Well, it's just . . . why don't you just go on? Why don't you make me know?"

"I don't know," he said. "This is better than nothing, I guess."

"You think I wouldn't like it."

"I didn't say that."

"But you do. That's it. You think I wouldn't like it."

"I don't know."

"You think there's something the matter with me." Her voice sounded cold now, too quiet.

"No. I didn't say that either," he said. "Hell, Laura, you get me all mixed up."

"Well, I'm all mixed up. Ever think of that?"

"It shouldn't be mixed up," he said stubbornly, putting all the blame on her as he always did. "Either you want me or you don't. That's all."

"That's not ever all," she said sadly.

He looked at her. "Chirk up, honey," he said. "Maybe it just takes time."

"I'm twenty-four years old," she said.

"Why don't you move out of that house?" he said suddenly.

"Why do you say that now?"

"It's just an idea."

"You don't like my family, do you?"

"I don't know them."

"Well, I don't like them much either, but they're mine. They live on what I make. There's nothing I can do about it. Oh, Carter, don't fuss with me. Don't let me fuss with you. That's all I do at home. Don't let me do it with you."

"O.K. No fussing. Let's go have a cup of coffee at Dupree's." He reached over and put his hand on hers.

"Julie's in there," Laura said when they started into the café.

"I thought you liked Julie."

"I do, but she makes me nervous. It's as though she sees through you into what you're thinking."

"Hell."

"Well, it's true. But I don't guess it matters. You like her, don't you?"

57

"She's a nice gal. She ought to marry Arlie."

"He's another one. He never says anything."

"He likes you."

"Oh, I like him too. It's just that he never says anything."

They went on into the restaurant. "Hi, chicks," Julie said, looking up. "Join the Saturday night sitters club."

They sat on stools next to her, and ordered coffee. "How's business?" Julie said.

"So-so. Hope to even out on the train tonight."

"Why don't you try round the poolroom? Bill was in while ago and said he had a big crowd tonight."

"Thanks. Maybe I will. You want to stay here, Laura, while I see if I can make a run or two down there? I'd just as soon not take you with that bunch."

"All right." Laura smiled at him. "I'll stay and talk to Julie and Estelle."

He touched her hair briefly. "See you in a little." He went out.

"That is one nice guy," Julie said.

"I know it," Laura said. "I really do know it. I don't know why I fuss with him."

"Do you?" Julie said. "But of course you would." She sipped her coffee. "I like you, Laura," she went on. "If I didn't think it'd put too much strain on our friendship I'd ask you a question."

Laura looked at her steadily. "The answer is, No, we haven't," she said.

"You in love with him?" Julie said.

"Dupree," Laura said. "Bring me some coffee, please." She turned and faced Julie. "Yes, I love him," she said.

Julie shook her head. "Well, it's none of my business," she said. "Only, one thing. Don't get to be too much of a symbol for him. That doesn't ever work, you know. Be his woman, even if you have to destroy something else."

"I don't understand you," Laura said.

"Call me Cassandra," Julie said. "Let's all walk down and talk to Arlie a while. Come on, Estelle. You can use the exercise."

"You been to college, Julie?" Laura said.

"A while. A long time ago."

"I went a while too," Laura said. "A long time ago."

"Come on, Es," Julie said.

From where he sat in the booth Will McCain watched them go out. "Goddamn," he said. "None of them so much as give you the time of day. I don't think they even knew I was sitting here."

"You say something, Will?" Dupree said. "You want to order?"

"Hell, no," Will said. He got up and went out of the café, almost running into Jackson Ferguson in the doorway. That's all I need, he thought. That's all the hell I need, to tangle with The Law.

It was nine o'clock. From the courthouse the clock boomed out suddenly, sending starlings into the air. The checker players on the courthouse lawn began folding their boards and stacking the men into boxes. The night was over for them.

It was dark in front of the poolroom. Carter went to the window and looked in over the green-painted lower half of the glass. The room was dim and smoky, the splashes of light from the shaded bulbs lighting up the white faces over the tables. He went in.

Bill Prince stood behind the half-counter watching the room. "Hi, Carter," he said. "Looking for business?"

Carter shrugged. He walked over and leaned his elbow on the counter, looking out over the room. "Got a crowd tonight, huh?" he said.

"Pretty good. Bunch from up around Holly Springs been in all afternoon trying to beat Jep Fleming. Then went and ate and came back and they're still at it. Don't know why folks don't learn nobody beats Jep."

"Anybody look like they need to go anywhere?"

Bill looked around the room. He appeared casual and uninterested in his customers, but he could tell you every person in the room, what they were doing, how many games they had played, and what they were likely to do in the next hour. "Couple fellows over yonder at the back table playing snooker," he said. "They're about half lit. Likely to want something more in a little."

"O.K.," Carter said. "I'll be outside." He went back out and sat in the darkened cab, watching the street. The poolroom was on a side street just off the square and not many people passed. He saw two telephone operators on their way to a late shift and Dupree's night waitress, hurrying by the poolroom, looking carefully in the opposite direction. He grinned. Annie was a fine one to look in the other direction from anything. She passed on around the corner and the street was still. A dog roamed the store fronts, looking for garbage, at the corner the traffic light burned red and green eyes onto the highway.

After a while the two men came out. One was short and fat. He stumbled on the door sill and his companion laughed. He was a little man, short and wiry. They both wore black-striped pants and white shirts. Carter tapped the horn and they looked toward the curb. "You need a taxi?" he said.

They came over to the car, peering in the window at him. The short fat man nudged the other in the ribs. "You wouldn't know where we could find a little, would you?" he said, snickering.

"Maybe."

The wiry man took over. "Do we have to pay you extra?" he said.

"I told you maybe I knew," Carter said. "If I did know I reckon it'd be worth something."

The man shrugged. "I reckon," he said. He pulled the other man aside and they talked together, swaying in the dim light from the poolroom. They came back to the cab. "How much?" he said.

"Five apiece."

They consulted again and got in the back seat.

Carter drove them to the back street garage apartment. "Right here?" one of them said. "This looks like a right nice neighborhood."

"It is," Carter said. "You better keep your voices down."

They looked at him and back at the apartment. "You better not be shaking us down," the small one said.

"It's all right," Carter said. He glanced up at the open window where a face appeared momentarily. "They know I brought you. Go on in."

The fat man took a ten-dollar bill from his pocket and handed it to Carter. "I don't guess you could come back and get us," he said.

Carter shook his head. "Not me. You just gave me the rest of the night off." He drove away, not waiting to see if they got up the nerve to go in or not.

Back on the square the movie was breaking. Ferguson

stood to one side, watching the crowd streaming out of the theater. He held his hand idly over his blackjack. Occasionally he turned to watch a car back out and go up the street.

Carter drove past him to the taxi stand. He parked and went over to where Herbert sat on the fence around the used car lot. Herbert looked up at him. "How'd you do tonight?" he said.

"All right. Sixteen bucks plus what Dupree pays me later. I'll let you know when I get it."

"You quitting?"

"Till traintime. It's my night to catch it, isn't it?"

"Yeah." Herbert wrote in his pocket-sized notebook. "Come on by after the train."

Carter took his guitar out of the car and rolled up the windows and locked the doors. He strolled up the street toward Arlie's, the guitar slung from one shoulder on its leather strap. When he came even with the gas station he saw Laura Lee's blonde hair and turned onto the concrete apron. They were standing around the Coke machine drinking Cokes and talking to Arlie, who sat in his straight chair propped against the wall. Carter walked around the building and stood behind them, still half in shadow. He propped his foot on an oil can rack and made a chord on the guitar.

Estelle turned toward him and screamed, a small bright sound in the night. Arlie's chair slapped down onto the front legs. "Good God!" he said.

Julie and Laura turned toward him, their faces pale in the light from the station. Julie laughed.

"I'm sorry," Estelle said. "You scared me. It's something about the way you looked, half in the dark like that with that guitar. It wasn't like you. It was—you know—real weird."

"Harlequin," Julie said.

Carter moved on into the light. "Close this joint up and let's go somewhere," he said.

"Too early," Arlie said. "You want me to lose money?"

"Let the boys keep her open then."

"Where we going? You got to meet the train, haven't you?"

Carter looked at his watch. "It's a good two hours," he said. "I just made a fast ten bucks. I'm taking off awhile."

Arlie grimaced. "You still making that run?" he said.

"When I have to."

Arlie shrugged. "Well, somebody's gonna make it."

"We could go down to the house," Estelle said. "There's some beer in the icebox." She looked at Julie worriedly.

"Why not?" Julie said. "Come on, Arlie. The boys can take care of things here."

"O.K." He got up slowly and walked across the concrete toward the tanks.

"Whose car we taking?" Estelle said.

"Better take mine, I guess—it's just down the street," Carter said. "We might stay till traintime."

Arlie came back toward them. "Lead on," he said.

"I got to stop a couple of places," Julie said when they were all in the car. "By the drugstore and by Dupree's."

Carter let her out in front of the café. "There's nowhere to park," he said. "I'll make the block and pick you up."

She went into the café. Dupree was standing over the grill frying hamburger steak. He reached over casually with his left hand and shook the potatoes that were frying in deep fat. Julie watched him for a moment, enjoying the clean quick movements with which he put a meal together. "You'd make somebody a good wife, buddy," she said.

Dupree turned. "Is Estelle all right?" he said.

"Right as rain. We're going to go down to your place awhile. I'll stay with her."

Dupree looked down at his hands and hastily turned the hamburger. "You're a good gal, Julie," he said softly. "You ought to stay here. Any town can use a few folks like you."

"Well, hell now, don't get me choked up," Julie said. "I'm going around to the drugstore and see if I can talk the pharmacist out of something for pain. She might need it later."

"Is she going to be all right?" Dupree said.

"Where'd you get the place?" Julie said.

"It's the one the nice folks here use," Dupree said. "I wouldn't send her nowhere else. It's the one the doctors know about."

"She'll probably be all right," Julie said. "How far . . ."

"Two months."

"She'll be all right. Try to calm down a little, huh? It'd

62

be a hell of a note if you started burning folks' supper."

Dupree turned from the grill and wiped sweat from his forehead onto a clean handkerchief. Then he turned back and dished the meat and potatoes neatly onto a plate with lettuce and tomato. "I'll call afterwhile," he said.

Julie went out and down the street to the drugstore. It was crowded, the booths full of high school kids, the usual quota of golfers sitting at the counter replaying the afternoon's game. She went by them and around the high counter at the back of the store. The Burke boy was on duty. He'd just completed his pharmacy course during the summer and he compounded prescriptions with a studied scientific care. "Hi, Burke," Julie said.

"Uh, hi, Miss Hobson. Can I help you?"

"Maybe. I got a friend in a little trouble. She might need some painkiller later. I haven't got and can't get a prescription."

"I don't know," he said.

"Where's the headman?" Julie said.

"You think he'd let you have it?"

"Yes."

"You wouldn't want much, would you?"

"No."

He moved bottles carefully across the countertop and peered around at the crowd in the front of the store. "What?" he said.

"Lemme see. She probably reacts like crazy to anything, so nothing very strong. I think just codeine."

"Oh. I guess I could let you have a few."

"I'm in a hurry," Julie said.

He counted the pills into a box and handed them to her. "You won't say . . ."

"Hell, boy, you're doing me a favor. What do you think I am?" She patted his cheek. "Give me something else to walk out with," she said.

"Oh. Yeah."

She reached around him and took a bottle of milk of magnesia and a bottle of aspirin off the shelf. She handed him a ten-dollar bill. "That cover it?"

"More than."

"Keep it." She walked out from behind the counter and past the eyes watching her in the mirror behind the fountain and out the door. Then she waited on the edge of the

63

sidewalk until she saw Carter's car come around the square.

The house where Estelle and Dupree Harris lived was in the south end of town. It was small and new and set precisely on a square green lawn. It was dark. Estelle fished a key out of her handbag and let them in. The house had the smell of disuse that houses slept in in the daytime always have. It smelled of stale food and stale sheets and airless discomfort. Estelle turned on a lamp. The base of the lamp was a purple horse studded with diamond dust. She had won it at the fair last year and was very fond of it. On the sofa were colored silk pillows with verses on them: To My Sweetheart and For My Pal. There was a thick layer of dust over all the furniture. "It's sort of in a mess," Estelle said.

Laura Lee sat down on the edge of the couch. Through an open door she could see into the kitchen, where dirty dishes were piled in the sink. She looked away.

"Let's all have a snort," Julie said. "Do you reckon you got a clean glass in this house?"

"I guess," Estelle said.

Julie went past her into the kitchen. She shook her head, moved the dishes out of the sink, poured in water and soap powder and dumped them back in. Then she rummaged the cupboards until she found five assorted glasses. "Come help me, Laura," she said.

Laura came slowly into the kitchen.

"Ice," Julie said.

Laura went to the refrigerator and took out the trays, looking for a place to put them down. Julie went past her and cleared the table, dumping the dishes in the sink. "Try that," she said.

Laura grinned. "I wasn't trying to be nasty," she said.

"I know it." Julie brought the glasses to the table and took the pint of whiskey out of her purse. "Relax, why don't you? You're among friends."

Laura put the ice carefully into the glasses. "What did you mean by what you said while ago?" she said.

"When?" Julie leaned back against the sink, watching her.

"In the café. About me and Carter."

"I don't know," Julie said. "Nothing."

"You think I ought to . . ."

"I don't think anything," Julie said, stirring the drinks. "I'm just an observer. Take these." She handed two of the glasses to Laura and expertly balanced the other three between her hands. They went into the living room.

Carter was sitting on a straight chair, strumming the guitar. Laura stood just inside the door for a moment, watching him. She could feel love for him like an alien presence in her, urging her on to him. And, at the same time, a revulsion, carefully ignored now and just as carefully looked at at certain times, alone at night. The revulsion had nothing to do with him. It was in herself, compounded of days and nights of living with revulsion, sounds and sights ignored since babyhood. Her mother. As always when Irene crossed her consciousness the revulsion flooded after it. She walked quickly across the room and handed Carter his drink. She took a long swallow of her own. She touched him, put her hand on his hair.

He looked up at her and smiled. She wanted to say, Help me, damn it. Help me. But she knew there was no telling him or explaining to him. He was in essence a stranger, as everyone was. It was no good. "You've got sweat on your face," she said harshly.

Once a long time ago when she had been seventeen one of them had come to the house, what her Aunt Olive had called a drummer, a huge red-faced man with ugly hands. She had never been able to stand ugly hands. He had kept trying to get her to sit in the kitchen with them. "You're so goddamned beautiful," he kept saying drunkenly. "You're so goddamned young." She had endured it, sitting on a kitchen chair carefully not looking at her mother sitting across from her, laughing, drinking gin straight out of a pale frosted bottle. Afterwards she had gone out to the yard and stood at the side of the house for hours staring up at the high impregnable stars. It was then she began to like the night. The stars were so far away, so untouched and untouching, so wonderfully perfectly clean.

Carter was watching her, the hurt bewildered look on his face. She felt contrite. "Play 'Fallen Star,'" she said.

He played it for her, singing the words softly under the accompaniment: *A fallen star, that's what you are. The twinkle in your eyes came from the sky. You must have strayed, from the Milky Way. A fallen star, that's what you are.* "Please don't cry," he said.

"I'm not crying."

"You are. You're crying inside where it don't show. Please don't cry."

"I never cry," she said. She drank the rest of the whiskey in one gulp.

Across the room Julie sat on the floor at Arlie's feet. She watched Laura and Carter quietly, sipping her drink. Estelle watched Carter. Her face was flushed and her hair tousled. She leaned back on the silk cushions. "Play 'Miller's Cave,'" she said. "I like that one."

Julie laughed. "You would, Essie. You would."

"I like the way it talks about Waycross, Georgia," Estelle said. "I was in Waycross once." She giggled. "But I never met the meanest man there."

"No," Julie said. "But if you did, Dupree'd probably kill him and end up just like the feller in the song."

"You reckon he would?" Estelle said, her voice raised in excitement.

They all laughed, even Laura. "Anybody else want a drink?" she said.

Arlie handed her his glass and she went to the kitchen. Behind her she could hear Carter playing "Miller's Cave" for Estelle. He was really very good, much better than a lot of them that played and sang for a living. Arlie had told her that they'd tried to get Carter to go to Nashville and get on the Grand Ole Opry, but he wouldn't do it. He said he sang for himself. He sang for her too. She brought the drinks back.

"You can do 'Pretty Polly' for me now," Julie said.

"I don't like that one," Laura said. "It gives me the willies."

"That's why I like it," Julie said. "The best one for that though is 'In the Pines.' I don't sleep good after that one."

"Carter doesn't play it much," Laura said.

"It's pure death image," Julie said.

"It's just a pretty song to me," Carter said. "Like all of 'em. You sing, Laura. Sing 'In the Pines' for Julie."

"I can't carry a tune," Laura said.

"You can," Carter said. "That's just some crazy idea you've got in your head."

"I can't carry a tune," she said stubbornly.

66

*Sing for Mr. Jones, Laura Lee. Sing "Harbor Lights."
She had a new white dress and a gold locket. Sing for Mr.
Brown, Laura Lee. Sing "Mexicali Rose."*

Arlie got up and fixed himself another drink. He could
drink steadily for hours with no apparent effect. Julie
watched him come back from the kitchen. "Something
bothering you tonight?" she said.

"No more'n usual. How long you figure to stick around
here?"

"I don't know. I've got to stay with Es."

"You taken her to raise too?"

Julie shrugged. "You get enough of my time."

"No."

"Tomorrow's Sunday," she said.

"All day long. You want another drink?"

"All right."

He went to the kitchen. "How you feel, Essie?" Julie
said.

"All right, I think. Sort of like I might be gonna have
the misery."

"Um-hmm."

Carter put his guitar down and held out his arms.
Laura Lee sat down in his lap. She put her head on his
chest and snuggled against him. She felt warm and
drowsy and secure. "Let's sit here like this forever," she
said.

"All right." He kissed the top of her head.

"I'm beginning to feel right rosé," Julie said. "Not to say
high."

"Don't all of you get tight on me now," Carter said. "I
still got a train to meet." There was a knock on the door.
"Who the hell is that?" Carter said.

"Maybe it's Dupree," Julie said. "But why would he
knock?" She got up and walked to the door, balanced
gracefully and delicately on her stockinged feet. She
opened the door.

"Hi," Will McCain said. "Ain't you gonna ask me in?"
He walked past Julie and sat down on the couch.

"Hello, penny," Julie said.

"Saw your car, Carter. Figured a party might be going.
Am I wrong?"

"Get him a drink, Julie," Carter said. "There's no other
way of getting rid of him that I can see."

"You talk tough, son," Will said.

"Get your drink, Will, and go on about your business," Carter said.

"Seems to me I've just evened up the party," Will said. "You folks were a man short." He looked at Estelle. "Damn, you look good," he said.

Estelle giggled. Arlie brought a drink and silently handed it to Will.

Will sat down beside Estelle and draped his arm across the back of the sofa behind her. She squirmed a little and he grinned at her. "Y'all will never guess what I've been doing," he said.

"Is it worth it?" Julie said.

"Well, it's right funny," Will said. He dropped his hand onto Estelle's hair.

Laura Lee sat up and slid out of Carter's lap. "I want another drink," she said. "Or do I?" She looked around the room and went over and sat down beside Julie. "I don't guess I do."

"Ain't anybody gonna ask me about it?" Will said.

"We figure we won't have to," Carter said.

Will took a drink, made a face, and moved his fingers in Estelle's hair. "Well. You remember those two guys from out of town that come by the station?"

"Yeah," Arlie said. "So?"

"The Law picked 'em up, by God. They come out to the house and got a pint. They were with a couple of local gals—that Charlene Webster and somebody. They pulled out of the road onto the highway, and they got 'em. They didn't see the gals till they had already stopped them, I reckon. Hell, it was the whole bunch of 'em: ole Will Graves from the highway patrol, that sheriff's nephew from his office, and one of the city boys. I tell you I'd have given a pretty to have seen their faces when they opened the doors and saw those local girls in there. They were all set to get that car, seeing those out-of-county plates.

"Mama and Uncle Jake were standing in the door watching and saw 'em. Lord, Mama like to had a fit. She said, 'I've gone and got those two nice little girls in trouble letting them have that whiskey. You just get in that truck, Will McCain, and get to town before they do.' She handed me a hundred-dollar bill out of her dress calm as

68

you please and said, 'If they take them to the jail, bail 'em out.'

"Well, I went down there, parked in front of the jail and waited, but they never did come. Way on afterwhile I see 'em cruising around the block, all that Law in a bunch. They stopped and passed the time of day with old Blackjack, so I drove off and looked around some. I didn't want to be caught that close to the jail. I finally run into the girls up at the drive-in and they told me about it. Said that Law piled out on 'em like the Marines landing, made 'em all get out of the car. Then Graves sees those girls and he sort of coughs and all the other guys look at them. Will Graves says, 'You folks was driving around up in bootleg territory. We gonna have to search the car.' Charlene Webster said she never saw three guys have to work so hard to keep from finding a pint of whiskey. They'd just thrown it up in the back and put a coat over it, and every one of them patted that coat and said, 'Nothing's here,' straight-faced as you please. I can't wait to tell the old man about it. Course I had to go out and tell Mama and give her back her hundred dollars. Uncle Jake laughed fit to bust. He said they'd have really all been sweating come next election if they hadn't recognized those girls in time."

Carter laughed. "I bet it killed you to take back the hundred," he said.

" 'Twasn't exactly the happiest thing in the world."

Estelle moved closer to Will. "You want to sweeten my drink, Will?" she said.

He took the glass, whispering something to her as he got up. They all watched him silently.

"You better get him out of here, Carter," Arlie said when Will went into the kitchen. "You know Estelle ain't the brightest thing in creation."

"I know it," Carter stood up. When Will came back into the room he walked over to him. "I think you better get on home, Will," he said.

"Who the hell are you telling what to do?" Will said.

"You," Carter said. "Estelle's tight. Leave her alone."

"I ain't doing nothing she don't want me to do," Will said. He walked over deliberately and sat down by Estelle. He put his hand on her waist and pulled her to him. "You want me here, don't you, pretty?" he said.

69

Estelle looked up at him. The tip of her tongue came out and moistened her lips. "Sure," she said slowly.

"Good God-almighty, Estelle," Julie said loudly. "Are you nuts?"

Estelle looked at her. "What's the matter, Julie?" she said. "I'm not doing anything. I was just flirting with Will a little. I always do." She frowned. "You all trying to break up a good party?"

Arlie stood up. He moved quietly across the floor. He put one hand under his arm and lifted Will off the sofa. With the other hand he took Will's left arm and twisted it behind him. Then he walked him across the floor to the door. "Good night, Will," he said quietly.

Will struggled against him but he couldn't break his hold. "You son-of-a-bitch," he said. "I'll kill you. Do you hear me? The first rotten chance I get I'll kill you."

"Go home, Will," Carter said. He stepped around Laura and Julie and stood behind Arlie. "And don't be calling friends of mine names," he added.

"I'll get you too," Will said. "Mr. High-and-mighty. Both of you. Think you know all there is to know about everything that is. I'll get both of you. See if I don't." He yelled the words into Arlie's face.

Arlie opened the door and pushed him onto the steps.

"Bastard," Will said. "Mother-loving bastard."

Arlie shut the door and shot the bolt. No one spoke.

"I wish you hadn't done that, Arlie," Julie said finally.

"What did you want me to do? Let him get himself killed? I can see Dupree walking in here . . ."

"It's even worse than that," Julie said. "But I still wish you hadn't. He means it. He hates you."

"He's all mouth," Arlie said.

Julie shook her head. "I don't like it."

Estelle was crying. "I'm sorry," she said. "I didn't mean to cause anything like that. I'm sorry."

"Oh, shut up," Laura Lee said suddenly. "Quit bawling. You knew exactly what you were doing and you're enjoying it right now."

Julie looked at Laura appraisingly. "Well," she said. "You decided to work up a little spirit, after all. It's right becoming to you. Look at her, Carter. She looks plum beautiful."

"I just don't like things like that," Laura said.

70

"Nobody else does," Julie said. "But they happen."

Arlie stood against the wall, a muscle in his cheek twitching.

"I'm sorry, Arlie," Carter said.

Arlie laughed, a harsh strained sound. "Hell, Carter, you can't help what you drew for a brother. None of us can help what we draw in the family lottery."

Laura looked at him. "But we can't get away from it either," she said.

"That's what they call karma," Julie said.

"Karma?" Arlie said. "What's it mean?"

"Your personal fate. What you drew you couldn't control."

"Don't seem to give us much of a go at it, does it?" Arlie said.

"That's only a part," Julie said. "You control what you do beyond it."

"Hell," Arlie said. "That's like running a race with a lead weight tied to your tail."

Julie laughed. "Ain't it the truth," she said.

"It's time for the train," Carter said. He moved across the room and put his hand down to Laura. She took it and pulled herself to her feet. "You going with us?" Carter said.

"Why not?" Julie said. "I don't want to hang around here right now anyway. Will might come back."

"He's not coming back," Arlie said.

Julie shrugged. "I'd rather go."

"O.K.," Arlie said. "We go."

They went out into the quiet of midnight. From the east the sound of the train whistle came on the hot night air. On the street corner the air was hazy with the wings of circling moths as they beat their frenetic way toward the core of brightness the single bulb made in the dark. Down the long hollow of the street each corner burned its spot of brightness into the pregnant night. Overhead the sky was filled with traveling light, the moment's glimpse of distant, cold, unseeing stars.

2.

HE could see the square from where he stood by the Sulphur Well. It was quiet now. The last of the wagons and pickups had driven away toward the highways and the sleeping fields. The picture shows were closed, presenting already to the empty streets the bill for Monday or the flat blank faces of empty billboards. The drugstores gave only blue and sleepy night lights onto the sidewalks in front of them. Across the street the Majestic still threw a red splash of life into the dark and across the intersection at the corner Machen's Filling Station was open. Farther down the street the circle of light from the taxi stand lighted up the parked cars in the secondhand car lot.

The train whistle sounded on the night air and he raised his head. The sound came from Holly Springs Crossing, five miles away. He shifted his blackjack on his side. Time enough to walk leisurely to the station.

A car came around the square, turning across the yellow parking spaces and going past him and on out of town. He looked after it, but it was gone before he could see the license plates. There were sounds in the stillness; an occasional burst of noise as a motor turned over suddenly from the highway, a car going slowly along the streets of town. He began to walk, hearing his footsteps behind him, clipped syllables of authority in the dark.

He went along the street past the poolroom. There was still light and noise here too, the muted click and shuffle, the dim tired voices. He looked in but he didn't go through

72

the door. At the corner he watched the highway, a long black ribbon of communication stretching northeast and southwest, tying Bellefonte reluctantly to the world. He crossed, and passed the silent lumber yards.

The station loomed up out of night, the small lights burning on the rafters. The mail truck, motor idling, stood beside the platform. Ida Jacks in her khaki britches and hip boots leaned against the side of it, waiting for the mail.

"'Do, Ida," he said.

She nodded, pitching her cigarette onto the gravel in front of her. "She's in the block," she said.

The town police car turned into the graveled space and stopped. The sheriff's nephew was in the front seat with Thurston Marlow, the other city deputy. Ferguson didn't look at them. He went to the station and leaned against the yellow board walls, watching the shining rails, remembering the sound they gave off even though it had been thirty years since he had laid his ear to them to hear it for himself.

If he could have afforded hate he would have hated Thurston Marlow, knowing the hate should not be directed toward Marlow at all but toward the town, toward the new smiling faces of the college graduates on the city council. But he couldn't afford hate, not for Thurston, not for the new order. He had to be careful, and hate destroys care. Bellefonte he could never entirely hate. It was his in the darkness, sleeping under his watch. He had to love it for its thralldom to him. While it slept he held it in his hands, while it slept the underlying dark of it was his: to protect, to save, and to banish and confine.

That was for now. That was until the city council smiled again and told him the whole force had to be mechanized. He waited for this day as one might await a sentence. He knew it would come eventually, but he refused to face that eventuality. It was nonsense anyway. No man in an automobile could watch that square as he could on foot. And it was the square where trouble began. It might ray out into the streets and roads and lawns, but here it began. The square, where he knew each shadow and jut of building, each car and face and walk. He moved around the station and looked up the track. Jackson Ferguson could not drive an automobile.

"The train's coming," Irene Colvin said. She stirred restlessly in the front porch rocker, straining her ears in the darkness, listening. Beside her on the plank floor was a half-empty fifth of blended whiskey. She tapped it with the edge of her foot and grunted. It was the last she had in the house, the last of what she'd brought from Newcastle last week when she'd gone shopping with Mrs. Butler. She'd hoped to save it, get a pint from McCain's for tonight. But Laura! Miss Laura couldn't even give her a few bucks. She could probably get whiskey for nothing, dating Carter McCain, but had she ever brought any home? Never. Laura. She picked up the bottle and drank from it, setting it back on the boards with a thump. From the upstairs window she could hear the snores of J.O., the long shuddering growl, followed by a short gasp, growing louder and youder until it became a sudden violent snort and he woke himself up. Then it would stop for a space of two minutes and begin again. She drank from the bottle.

She had had a red dress once, with an overskirt of ecru lace, and red satin shoes to match. That was in the time when they threw stockings away when they got dirty. She could still feel the way the silk wisps felt in your hand, crumpling them into a ball and tossing them casually into the wastebasket. They weren't wasted, of course. The cook got them and took them to her daughter to wear—with a razor in the top, she guessed. It amused her to think of her discarded hose with a razor in the top. She laughed aloud.

"You ought to marry Mr. Colvin," her mother had said. "Such a distinguished man. So much family, dear—and money. Though that really isn't too important. You would like Bellefonte. It's such a pleasant town. I was in school with Buz Mayhill from there, you know. Such *nice* people in Bellefonte. I still have a recipe from Aunt Caroline McCloud. She used to give them for wedding presents, only one to each girl, each different. You were to guard the secret of them with your life, and pass them on to your own daughters. You'll get it, of course. It's the Sally Lunn, a real prize. She took a fancy to me at a party once and sent it, even though they seldom get out of the town."

Irene remembered writing a grocery list on the back of that recipe and misplacing it somewhere. Laura had been furious with her about that. Laura was such a little prig. She wondered what on earth that taxi driver saw in her.

He certainly looked as though he'd be interested in something more than Sally Lunn handed down. She stirred uneasily in her chair. She could hear the train coming into town now. It sounded very loud in the quiet. It even drowned out J.O.'s snores.

Will McCain was driving his uncle Jake back to town. He sat stonily beside him, looking squint-eyed through the windshield.

"Something the matter with you, boy?" Jake said.

"Nah." He pressed his foot harder on the accelerator.

"Just in a hurry?" Jake said.

"Yeah."

They covered the silent highway in a swoop and rattle and ran the red light coming into town.

"What you think about Carter and little Colvin?" Jake said. He leaned back against the seat and pushed his battered hat back.

Will made a small disgusted sound.

"That way, huh?" Jake said. "Seems a nice little girl to me."

"Snotty," Will said shortly. A car darted out onto the highway in front of him and he slammed viciously at the brake, throwing Jake forward.

Jake leaned back again. "Seems nice to me," he said calmly.

"You like everybody," Will said.

Jake laughed. "I reckon," he said. "Too much trouble to dislike 'em. Makes you miserable all the time. Like you . . ."

"You keep your nose out of my business," Will said.

Jake shrugged. "Always have," he said.

Will sighed. "Yeah. I guess you have," he said. "Sorry. Where you want out?"

"Up the café, I guess. Shank of the evening."

Will pulled into the empty space in front of the restaurant. "Look at that s.o.b. in there, dishing up his hamburger," Will said. "With a looker like Estelle sittin' home alone."

"That what's bothering you?" Jake said. Then quickly, "Sorry. No prying."

Will turned to face him. "What I really want," he said. "The paratroopers, Uncle Jake. How about that, huh?"

75

"If you were mine I'd say yes," Jake said. "They'd work the damned pants off of you and you'd be too tired to get into anything. Yep. If you were mine I'd say yes."

"Why don't you talk to Mama?" Will said. "She always listens to you."

Jake shook his head. "You just got the one year of school," he said.

"Oh, hell. Let's grab a cup of coffee." Will got out of the pickup.

Jake followed him slowly. "I hear the train coming in," he said. "You not going over?"

"I haven't lost nothing over there," Will said.

"I just like trains," Jake said. "Back when ole Clint Riley used to drive 'em I used to go long with him sometimes. Just for the ride, you know."

Will turned toward him, his hand on the door. "Riley?" he said. "That ole coot lives over in niggertown?"

"Yeah," Jake said. "He was quite a driver in the old days. Could get more out of a steam engine than anybody I ever saw. Never went for the diesels though. Let 'em retire him after they came in. Said he never could get used to them somehow."

"You know that old guy?" Will said.

"Why sure I do," Jake said, puzzled. "Some reason that surprises you?"

"That's where that Julie stays," Will said uncertainly.

"Yeah. Go in in, boy," Jake said. "I need a little coffee."

Will opened the door. He looked over his shoulder at Jake. "What's she doing over there?" he said.

"Who?"

"Julie. You know those folks. What's she doing over there?"

"None of my business," Jake said.

"But you know, don't you?" Will said.

"I didn't say that." Jake walked past Will and sat down at the counter. "Hello, Dupree," he said.

Will sat down by him. He looked at him closely, his eyes narrow and yellow in the sudden light. "But you know, don't you?" he said.

"Gimme a cup of java, Dupree," Jake said.

Midnight. The time between. Here the night divides along an axis. Here the timid and the demi-dark go home.

To close the blinds and light the lights and find the beds, to shed bright clothes and paint like chrysalides, to lock the doors and wind the clocks and close the eyes. Afterwards it will be morning, the stretch of dark that reaches toward dawn and daylight. What's left out now belongs out, or wants to. Closed out with the cats and morning damp. Soon now last slams of doors and last good nights. By one o'clock the flurry will subside and day people sleep. A few of them hurry home now on the midnight train.

Carter swung onto the gravel by the station, tapping his horn to Thurston Marlow, the deputy. They had a friendly rivalry. The police met the midnight train and took home anyone who needed a ride. Those left over, the ones there was no room for or who preferred not to ride with The Law, even to home and bed, went to the taxi. The train trip rotated among the drivers nightly. On some nights there were no fares at all, on others one or two. Some nights there were enough for The Law and the taxi alike. After a concert or a ball game in Chattanooga it was lucrative. At Christmas it always paid off to meet the train. Two girls Carter knew always brought their Christmas whiskey back on the midnight train in a shopping bag. They did this so The Law could carry it home for them. It had become a ritual with them, buying the gaily packaged fifths and stuffing them under the Christmas gifts, allowing Thurston Marlow to gallantly carry the shopping bags to the city police car and to the house for them when they reached home.

Arlie parked beside him. They had stopped to pick up Arlie's car in case he got some fares. It wasn't likely, Carter thought. Not on an August night.

From his place beside the station Jackson Ferguson watched them, seeing the easy gesture Carter made toward Thurston. His mouth tightened. This was the new law, friends to the bootlegger and the taxi driver. He turned back and watched the train come into view down the waiting track.

Ida Jacks had already adjusted the mailsack on the post in case the train had no passengers to disembark or pick up and therefore didn't stop. There was still no one on the platform except Ferguson, so she watched to see if the train was slowing; it was. She stepped back and wait-

77

ed. For many years Ida's husband had been the mail-train man. When he died she had taken his job, over loud protests. She had eight children and she had to feed them. She hoisted the heavy sacks and carried the locked mail into the post office with a care and patience her husband had never shown. After the first year they had ceased to think of her as a usurper of male rights and been glad to keep her. She was the best mail-truck man they'd ever had.

The silver train slid into the station, the green-curtained windows closed against the night. The conductor climbed down and helped the passengers descend. An old lady, clutching an ancient round hatbox and a string shopping bag of colored packages—Mrs. Compton Henry, come from Roanoke to help her daughter birth her third baby; three girls from the music academy in Chattanooga, home for a surprise Sunday visit; a stranger in a snap-brim hat and a Dacron suit.

Jackson Ferguson placed the old lady and the three girls tidily in his memory. Then he looked at the stranger. He studied him for a moment, casually. The man turned and walked past him. Jackson straightened up. He moved away from the side of the station and stood watching the man as he picked his finicky way along the gravel. He watched him walk through the bright light from the pole where Ida Jacks was hefting the mailbags into the waiting truck and step down off the platform into the shadows. He nodded a little. The man did not approach either the taxi or the police car. He walked away into the darkness of the street, toward town.

Ferguson stood still looking after him for a moment. Then he stepped off the platform and began to walk toward the square himself. He knew who Julie Hobson was, suddenly, like a small flash of sheet lightning on the horizon of memory. Now he needed the time to know what he was going to do with the knowledge. Behind him the lights of the station faded into the dark; ahead of him the street lights of town burned quietly. He reached the edge of the square and began his circuit of the block, walking slowly and carefully, his blackjack slapping gently against his muscled leg. The stranger was nowhere in sight.

78

Julie wasn't surprised to see Bagley get off the train. She hadn't expected him so soon, but she wasn't surprised. She looked at Arlie, sitting beside her in the car, and she tried very hard not to care. After a few minutes she was very sure she didn't. She continued to watch the silver and green train, starting to move now, slowly, down the tracks away from the station. In just a few moments it was gone, the small red and green lights hurrying away into the darkness toward Hunter City, leaving only an old lady with presents for the grandchildren, three girls with dreams behind their painted faces, and a tall thin man in a Dacron suit.

She had been born in the Tidewater region of Virginia. Earliest memories, walking barefoot where the sand was damp, picking the flotsam from the littered beach, watching black branches left by southern winds. And the smell, that smell of salt and sand and clean wide spaces that followed her even here and now—the only homesickness for anything she had ever known.

Her father had been a lawyer, a tall man remembered in a dark small office where the litter covered everything. They lived in a rambling gray and white house where the litter from the office overflowed. There were always stacks of briefs, books tumbled from the shelves and left to lie where they had fallen, newspapers and magazines and yellow pages of scrawled undecipherable notes; the smell of apples lying half-rotted in wooden bowls, and the sharp sweet smell of early mint.

She had loved her father. He had been a part of the sea and the sand and the shore-swept days. She came to his office in the afternoons after school at Miss Couch's Academy for Girls, the straight white building set behind the high iron fence, where she was taught to sing and dance and play the piano, to paint and sew and incidentally to read and write and cipher. Her father taught her history and the story of mankind. He would read to her in the late afternoon light, from a book picked at random from the piles and stacks of books in that cluttered office. Shakespeare maybe, or *The Decline and Fall*, or Greek mythology, whatever came to hand, whatever his mood of the afternoon.

He drank. She knew that because she loved the smell of bourbon that always lingered about him, the smell that

79

made her mother, Missy, wrinkle her nose and go away onto the veranda to fan with the white lace fan that looked so ridiculous with her print house dress.

"Look at the two of you," she would say. "Go wash that face, Julia. And plait your hair. Supper's almost ready already." And in the summers, "Where *are* your shoes?"

On the weekends they went to the beach, her father wearing a disreputable pair of khakis and a battered felt hat which he kept hidden in the office for fear Missy would give them to the yardboy. They would walk for miles along the tideline picking up shells and seaweed and flotsam, making a world out of a world, bringing the sea onto the shore. They would eat supper at John's Fish House, a ramshackle wooden building on the pier where the water winked up through the cracks in the floor and the smell was fish and sea and spilled beer. It was owned by John Caple, an old schoolmate of her father's who had given up in his senior year at the university and come home to fish. When they got home Missy would make them undress on the screened back porch and go up the back stairs to bathe.

Her father died when she was twelve years old. She had gone by after school as always to find him slouched over the desk, his hands on the open book in front of him, Bertrand Russell. She had stood there in the doorway, knowing before she approached the desk, putting out a hand to touch the already cold hand in front of her. Then the running, out the door and onto the beach, running for miles along the tideline, until night came and John Caple found her, huddled on a rock below the pier, and brought her gently home.

Afterwards her mother opened the boardinghouse. There was a little money and that is what she did with it, bought the old Anderson place that overlooked the beach and painted and papered and set the rockers on the long porch and put the nice little ads in the *Saturday Review*. She was so busy after that, Missy Hobson. It was as though for years she had lived in the warm litter of some huge alien beast and now she was free again to be Miss Clairmont in a lavender dress. There was never any litter in the Beachcomber—that sad inappropriate name, chosen by God-knew-whom or for what purpose. The boardinghouse was as clean and spick and span and devoid of life as a surgery. In the kitchen pots gleamed on painted walls, in the bathrooms linen was changed daily down to the bathmats. On the porch the smell of floor cleaner, laced with insect repellent, killed forever the smell of salt and sand.

Through the clean airy rooms Missy moved, directing, planning, smiling, making the guests from up east feel at home, wearing her afternoon frocks with her afternoon smile, her hair crimped twice weekly at the beauty parlor downtown against the salt wind.

The old gray house was sold to a man who put a filling station on the lot. After the irresistible impulse to walk by there once Julie never went through that part of town again.

In the forties the war came to them; the surge of khaki and blue moved across the landscape with its own alienness. Missy chose to ignore the war. There was a neat black and white sign tacked to the front porch railing. No Servicemen. Missy had escaped untidiness; she was not going to fall prey to it again.

The sailor saw Julie in John Caple's fishhouse. She was sitting on a stool, swinging her feet against the bar and drinking a forbidden beer. She was eighteen then, tall and brown, with startling green eyes in a tan face. The sailor saw Missy's neatness in her, the smooth plaits across the head, the freshly ironed blue dress. But he saw too the bare feet and the long colt legs, the quiet shine in the green eyes when she looked up at him.

He was only twenty years old and he was John Caple's nephew, stationed at Norfolk and spending a forty-eight-hour pass with his uncle. He walked across the board floor and sat down by her.

With the exception of old John Caple, he was the first person she'd felt easy with since her father died. She fell in love with him. And because Missy had taught her that it could not be done without marriage she married him.

She spent two nights with him in a small crowded room in a motel before Missy found them, two nights that became as much a part of her as the sound of the sea outside the window. But when Missy came for her, she went. Because she hadn't expected anything else. She had learned to believe that nothing you really want ever lasts. The third night she spent in her own white bed while

81

Missy, using the legal knowledge she had acquired and remembered quite well from the days of Henry Hobson, had the marriage quietly annulled. But she couldn't annul the two days and nights in the grimy motel. Those two days were not part of the neat erasable world of Missy Hobson.

Lying in the white bed in the white room she heard John Caple come to the house, heard him talk to Missy, heard him go away defeated. She didn't cry. She never cried again after the day alone on the beach when she knew her father was gone forever. This had been only a repetition of that loss, another failure of the world to meet the needs of Julie Hobson. After this time she didn't expect anything at all.

She held out for the University of Virginia. Missy wanted Bryn Mawr, but with a quiet stubbornness Julie won. She took a liberal arts course. The first year she went with a law student, but she never found anything in him to remind her of the quiet man in a littered, brief-strewn office, nor even, except when he was very drunk and forgot himself, of the sailor Jack Caple. Later there was an English major, a naval veteran. He drank, but there was no gentleness in him. After that she ceased looking even for that.

At the end of two years she accepted the offer of a trip to Jamaica where she shared a beach cottage with a homosexual art major who wanted to paint her. His name was Tommy and she liked him. He was the first person she had liked in a long time, but he depended on her, so that there is an unbelievably blue and green and sunlit land she was more than ever alone.

She met Brad Tanner at the new shining glass and brick American hotel that sprawled and towered simultaneously on the primitive lovely soil like a prison block in Paradise. He was a card dealer, a tall handsome man who attracted her the first night she saw him, watching her across the glitter of the blue free-form pool. There was something about him like Jack Caple, but nothing like her father. What attracted her was the obvious footloose quality about him. He moved on; he never stayed for good. She saw this in him before he touched her. And later, in the cool moist air of Mandeville where she had come with him to watch the races she knew she was going to follow him. For by now she had faced the one real thing in herself; she couldn't stop running. She hadn't stopped since the day she'd run out the door of her father's office. The two days with Jack had only been possible because she knew Missy would come and take her away from him, take her away and shut her up so that she would have the need and opportunity to run again.

Then there was Vegas and Monte Carlo, and a dirty sad place in Mexico, and a weird waiting time in the heat of Venezuela. And once, like the air of home, six months on the island of Majorca, where the sea was outside the window and the salt smell drifted all day long while she slept. For by that time she was of the night and the sun signaled the time of sleep.

It was in Monte Carlo for the season for the fourth time that she knew she could no longer stand the smell of the sea. It was a blue day, with sun. She had gotten up in the middle of the afternoon, coming down to the casino early, watching the daytime players with a slight curiosity, holding the first drink in her hand. A man standing next to her at the dice table remarked casually, "It was snowing when I left New York." And there in her mind were close white skies and blinding cold with the snow coming out of the world around her, holding her in a soft cold dream of cleanliness. That day, ten years ago, she found Missy's love of neatness still alive and strong in her tropic-trained body, and she stopped. Stopped chasing the sea and sun and went home with the friend of Brad's, home to the fur coat and the clean apartment above the neat clean New England street, and thought she had found a place to stay. Now, watching the train going away into the dark, into the distance, into another place, she knew how she had betrayed herself. She had accepted this false security, this false peace, for the same basic reason. It was a form of running. For as long as she stayed with the man she lived with now, for as long as she remained a part of him, she was running, no matter how permanent, no matter how secure the street address. She hadn't stopped at all, and now she never would. The desire to wouldn't be enough now. It had become the way she existed—the only way she could.

"Let's go, Arlie," she said to the man beside her. "The train's gone."

"Where to?" he said.

"Follow Carter. He picked up the old lady."

"All right." Arlie backed out and followed the bouncing taillight of Carter's cab back through town and out to the lakefront. They left the old lady with her presents on the steps of the white ranch house and turned in the driveway and drove back toward town.

On the edge of a field before the dirt road reached the highway Carter stopped. Arlie pulled up beside him. "Where now?" he said.

Carter shrugged. He looked at Laura sitting beside him and at Estelle, white and quiet on the other side of Laura. "Coffee?" he said.

Julie shook her head. "It's not time for that yet," she said. "What about your place, Arlie?"

"It's not cleaned up," Arlie said.

"Oh, Christ! I'll clean it." She turned her face toward the window, looking out at the weed-choked fields beside the dirt road. Somewhere a cow lowed, softly and rhythmically. The smell of hay was on the air. It was still, the dark lying across the country, hiding everything that wasn't soft and gentle and waiting. "Oh, hell," Julie said.

Arlie looked at her. "Blackjack'll see us," he said.

"Wait till he's on the other side of the square," she said. "He never sees you and me."

"There's not this many of us," Arlie said.

"I'm not going back down to Estelle's," Julie said quietly.

"Will ain't going to do nothing. I told you," Arlie said.

"Your place," Julie said stubbornly. She didn't look at him.

"All right." He motioned Carter to follow them and pulled out onto the highway.

In town Kermit Bagley walked the two blocks to the Vance Hotel. He went in and took a single room with a window overlooking the highway. He laid the articles from his pockets in a neat pattern on the dresser and took off his suit. Then he went into the bathroom and dipped the suit expertly in the lavatory and hung it neatly on a hanger from the shower-curtain rod. He buffed his shoes with a towel and hung his hat neatly on the lampshade. Then he climbed into bed. In two minutes he slept soundly.

school kid. I couldn't make that one out so I says, 'Well, do you?' and he says, 'Yeah. Sure. You know where you want to go, I reckon.' The truck driver says, 'You drive your jitney buddy, and I'll tell you where to go,' and he sort of flexes his muscles. Well, the driver pipes down then and drives us on out of town, past all them slag heaps and junk yards and what not around Newcastle. Then we were out in the open country coming down 36, so I knew where I was: on the way to Druid City on the four-lane. All that country air sobered me up some and I was beginning to wonder what this guy had got me into when all of a sudden the driver just turned off the road into what looked like a cornpatch. I didn't see no road nor nothing but corn. I says, 'What's coming off here?' and that driver says, 'You said the Broadway Plaza, didn't you?' And I thought, O.K. so the Broadway Plaza's in the middle of a cornpatch. It crossed my mind this driver and the truck fellow was in cahoots and fixing to roll me, but it didn't figure. 'Cause the jitney idea had been mine right along. So I didn't say nothing and in a minute I saw that there was a kind of road through the corn. Not much of one, but cars had been over it before. It still looked funny to me but I began to figure maybe the trucker was pimping for a bunch of dames out here in the cornpatch or something and I'd just got suckered in. So I rode with it.

"In a few minutes I saw some lights ahead. No blaze of 'em, mind you, but enough to know there was something out there. Then I could see a long white house in the middle of the fields. There were a few electric bulbs screwed into the rafters, which meant, I figured, it wasn't any private residence. It looked like one, just the same. There was some cars parked around, but it looked like an ordinary white farmhouse built out of concrete blocks and a little batten board. The driver says, 'Want me to wait?' And the guy with me says, 'We'll get a ride back. What do I owe you?' I let him pay. I figured this was his party.

"We got out and stood there a minute in the corn, looking at the house. There was noise from inside, sounded like a phonograph playing and some dancing. I was cold sober by then, and looking over my shoulder. Moon was shining like crazy on the fields.

" 'Come on,' this guy says and we went around to what

87

looked like the side door and went in. So help me, what we went into was an ordinary farmhouse bedroom—Sears Roebuck bedroom suite, big wardrobe, linoleum on the floor, cedar chest with a Teddy bear sitting on it. That's right, a kid's Teddy bear, and not one of those things to put on the bed either, a plain ole beat-up dirty Teddy bear. 'Looks like we made a mistake,' I said, and just then this feller in overalls puts his hand out and says, 'Two bucks apiece.' I gave him the money. By this time I'd have given him twenty just to find out what the hell was coming off. This guy with me he says, 'Come on, in here,' and we went through the door into the living room.

"Well, by God, there it was. That living room looked like nothing I ever saw before in my life. It was an ordinary living room, farmhouse furniture, linoleum rug, straight chairs, and in the corner an old-fashioned phonograph with a stack of 78 records. But that room, that farmhouse living room, was just full of queers.

"I just stood there and stared. So help me God, they were dancing with each other and sitting around on the Sears sofa in each other's laps, and draped around on the floor feeling each other up.

"That damned truck driver that had got me into this starts plain screaming at 'em. He says, 'Hellooo, Jere. Darling! Sweets!' And more of the same. Then he just prances off and leaves me standing there looking at the farmer.

" 'We have some whiskey in the kitchen,' he says to me in a country voice, and I says, 'You lead on, buster. I need it.' We picked our way through the living room and went into the kitchen. There was a worn-out looking woman sitting there guarding the whiskey. She had a stack of paper cups and some lemon slices and Seven-Up and Coke, and a bottle. She was doling it out in the paper cups fifty cents a throw. I got me a drink and looked down and there was a kid about seven or eight wandering around taking it all in. There was another one about three—this one a girl—sitting by the phonograph listening to the music. I had me about three of those paper-cup highballs in rapid succession. By this time the old farmer was beginning to think I was just slumming so he starts talking confidential to me.

" 'This is just a little place where some of the boys can

get together,' he says to me. 'Don't do no harm. Nobody'll have 'em anywhere else. They can come here and do a little drinking and dancing. No harm done.' 'Yessir,' I says. He put his hand on the little boy's head. 'This is my boy,' he says. 'Luke. He's a fine one, ain't he?' 'Yessir,' I says. 'Do you reckon I could have another one of those paper-cup jobs?'

"The old gal fixes me a drink and then she sort of frowns up at me and says, 'Son, you don't look like you got tendencies.'"

Julie came away from the window, laughing. "Arlie, you dog, I don't believe a word of it," she said. "That's the damnedest thing I ever heard of, and I've been a hell of a lot of places and seen a hell of a lot of things."

"It's the God's truth," Arlie said. "Kids and all. The God's truth. I sat around there in the kitchen drinking up the private stock while the ole gal told me they needed some newer records, and the little girl curled up on the floor and went to sleep, and the boys out front got a little louder and a little wilder, and finally this guy I came with sort of whoops out, 'Where is that sweet thing I brought out here with me?'

"'Is there a back door to this place?' I asked the ole lady. She sort of pointed over her shoulder and I went out of there. I didn't know where the hell I was or how the hell I was going to get back to town, but I took out across the cornpatch and after a while I came to the highway and hitched me a ride with a guy hauling fruit. When I saw what he was loaded with I just broke up. I whooped and hollered and laughed all the way back to Newcastle. The rest of that week I'd be driving along the road and I'd suddenly think of the look on that farmer's face or the way that woman said, 'You don't look like you got tendencies,' and I'd go off again. What I ain't figured out to this day is where the hell that ole farmer got the idea. Was he just sitting around one year when the crop failed, thinking, How'm I gonna make the feed money this fall? And just suddenly had a vision? Damned if I know. I've thought about it ever once in a while since and I've never thought how he could have got the idea. And even after he did how did he manage to advertise?"

Carter looked at Laura. She was laughing, all the way,

eyes, mouth, mind. He tightened his arm around her. "Arlie's quite a storyteller, isn't he?" he said.

She nodded. "It's the *way* he tells it," she said. "I've never heard anything like it."

"Arlie," Estelle said. "What did you say that truck you hitchhiked on was loaded with?"

"Fruit," Arlie said. They all laughed again.

"I got to have a drink on that," Julie said, going toward the kitchen.

Arlie got up and followed her. "They gonna stick around here all night?" he said.

Julie shrugged. A small frown appeared between her eyebrows. "I don't know," she said. "I guess till Dupree can get away anyway."

"Well, Estelle do complicate it," Arlie said. "We can't just choose up and go into another room and leave her sitting there."

Julie shook her head impatiently. "Arlie . . ."

"Yes ma'm."

"I'm going to have to talk to you tonight anyway."

"Yes ma'm?"

"Oh, dammit. I want you."

He pulled her against him. "It's mutual, you see."

"I'll think of something." She stepped around him and took the drinks back to the living room.

Under the bright lights of the café Jake had begun to feel drowsy. It was an odd thing for him. He never felt drowsy at night. It worried him. He had another pull at the bottle while Dupree's back was turned. The café was almost empty. It wasn't late enough for the truck drivers or the morning shift from the bedspread factory. Will sat impatiently on the stool beside him, drinking coffee. There was something Will wanted from him, but Jake couldn't put his finger on what it was. He got that way sometimes now after he'd been drinking steadily for several days. Things had a blurred feel to them. He could detect the motives but not the actuality.

He'd never much liked Will. Not as he did the rest of his brother's family. There was something in Will that frightened him. Ruthlessness. Luckily there didn't seem to be any power to go with it. But he'd always been afraid the chance might come. When the chance falls right,

90

there is no need of power. When the chance falls, ruthlessness is quite enough.

"You want some of my whiskey, boy?" Jake said. He'd never offered Will a drink before but he suddenly felt the need to see him vulnerable. He held out the half-empty bottle.

Will shook his head. "I'm thinking," he said.

The door opened and Jake put the pint hastily into his pocket. Ferguson came into the café. Will sat watching while he sat down on the end stool and drank his coffee.

"What you so interested in The Law for?" Jake said.

"I told you," Will said. "I'm thinking."

Jake shrugged. He leaned over to sip his coffee and around him the colors of the café seemed to dissolve suddenly into a kaleidoscopic pattern. "I think . . ." he said slowly. "Will . . ."

Dupree was suddenly standing beside him. "What's the matter, Jake?" he said.

Jake shook his head. "Nothing," he said. "It couldn't be bad whiskey. I get it from my own brother." He leaned forward onto the counter and shut his eyes.

Betty Dawson kept the desk in the emergency room of the new county hospital. It was a good job; there was very little business. Most of the time she read magazines and worked crossword puzzles out of a dollar crossword puzzle book she'd bought in Hunter City. Of course, when they did come in she had to assist in surgery, but she'd gotten used to it. For a long time she hadn't thought she'd be able to, but she learned. It was a trick really, a trick of the eye and ear. You had to quit looking at the person and watch the area being repaired. During the last year she'd even developed a sort of pride in the quickness and firmness of the motions with which she put the instruments in the proper place and carried away the waste products.

She was all right unless Dr. Kent was in surgery. Then she couldn't keep her eyes and ears impartial and when she opened them to let Dr. Kent in the other followed—the area being repaired became a boy's left arm or a girl's forehead. Her motions were still firm and quick and efficient but afterwards she couldn't go back to the magazines and crosswords. She didn't think she really wanted to be

91

a nurse. But she didn't see any doors opening any other way. Dr. Kent, for instance, was married and the father of three children. All of this was quite important to him and the early dawn hours she spent with him in a fishing cabin on the lake had nothing to do with it. She thought often of going away—to Newcastle, or Hunter City—but the thought of a big hospital frightened her. And, more simply, she didn't want to leave the dawns on the lake. So she worked at night and slept through the glare of day. And lived at dawn. *A two-letter word for sun-god—Ra.*

She heard the car drive into the ambulance entrance and got up, thinking it was one of the doctors. Then she heard the sounds the voices made on the night air and she knew it was an emergency after all. She went to the door.

Dupree Harris appeared in the entrance, holding Jake McCain in his arms. The old man looked frail and vulnerable with his battered felt hat missing and his eyes closed. Betty stared at him for a moment, then pushed a button on her desk. By the time the floor nurse came she'd taken Jake's pulse and talked to Dupree and put in a call for Dr. Kent, who was taking emergencies tonight.

They went down the hall with Jake and she turned to Will McCain, who was still standing by the desk watching her. "What's the matter with him?" he said.

She shrugged. "Looks like cardiac to me," she said. "I couldn't say until the doctor looks at him."

"He was just sitting there," Will said. " And keeled over. Damnedest thing I ever saw." He sat down on the edge of the desk. "I haven't seen you around in ages," he said. "You work all the time at night?"

She nodded. "You know I worked here as a D.O. student my last few years in high school, so I got through nursing school a lot quicker than most." She smiled at him. "I already knew about tender loving care."

"I knew you hadn't been out of school long," Will said. He got up and went to look out the window. "What's keeping the doctor?" he said.

"He lives all the way out on the point," Betty said.

"A hell of a place for a doctor," Will said.

"A good place for somebody who makes enough money."

"I better go on down there." Will turned toward the hallway, then stopped. "You know Carter?" he said.

She nodded.

"Think you could get hold of him someway? Try the taxi stand, the café, around? I reckon he ought to be here."

"Here's the phone," Betty said. "You call him."

"I don't want to call him," Will said. "But I reckon somebody ought to let him know." He walked on out of the room.

Dupree met him in the hall. "They're trying to make him comfortable," he said. "I guess I better get back downtown. Annie might not be able to handle things long."

"All right," Will said. "Maybe you can get Carter out here. I don't want to call Mama less I have to."

They watched Dr. Kent come into the hall, walking quickly, nodding, going past them into the room where Jake lay on the white bed.

"I'll get somebody out here," Dupree said. He went down the hall and out the door.

Will stood looking after him. "This is the goddamnedest night I ever spent," he said aloud. He felt sore and tired, almost as though he'd been in a fight. The sound of Arlie's and Carter's voices, forcing him out into the night, still echoed around him, and in spite of the confusion of Jake's attack and the genuine regret he felt for him, there was still the driving anger in him, the need to hit back. And there was nothing to hit. Whatever he might do to Carter or to Arlie was hidden, quiet in the dark, waiting. Now this had taken his time to think. He made a small noise and Betty Dawson appeared at the end of the hallway. "You all right?" she said.

"Sure, baby," he said. "Sure." He walked down the hall and into the reception room and sat on the edge of her desk again. "Why ain't I ever noticed how good-looking you are?" he said.

"I keep pretty busy," she said.

He watched her eyes. "I could keep you busier."

"I doubt it."

"I could try."

She moved toward him. It had been a long time since anyone had noticed her. Everyone around the hospital

93

knew she belonged to Charles Kent. She thought of the way Charles had brushed by her, interrogating her with raised brows. When she'd said, "Cardiac, Room 104, Jake McCain, Alcoholic," he'd reached out and pinched her and said, "That's my baby. All the facts." He always did this, but suddenly it angered her. She looked at Will McCain. He was a little young, but he was good-looking. "You stay up late nights too?" she said.

Herbert Winston had told Betty Dawson that he'd get Carter. He put the phone down and stood for a minute looking up toward the square. He knew where Carter was, he'd seen him go into Arlie's, but he hated to go up there and he hated to phone him the news. Carter was with his girl. Herbert didn't believe in getting into the private lives of the drivers. It made for trouble. There were enough arguments about who got to cruise and who stayed at the stand. He tried to keep a regular schedule rotating so that the same ones weren't stuck at the stand on Saturdays and so that a different guy got the train every night, but some of them were always bitching about it anyway.

He strolled up the street toward the corner, debating going on to Arlie's. He knew Carter'd be by later to settle up and he didn't actually know how serious it was with Jake. Evidently the hospital didn't either, yet. Jake had been drinking himself into the grave for years now, so it might be the big one. Still, you couldn't tell.

While he debated, standing irresolute in the circle of light, Carter and Laura came down the steps and got into Carter's car. Herbert waved, running toward them, but Carter only waved back and drove on. Herbert cursed briefly. He started on up the street toward Arlie's, but changed his mind. He didn't want to bother Arlie Machen at two in the morning. Arlie had never been anything but pleasant to Herbert, or to anybody else that he knew of, but he didn't want to annoy him. There was something about Arlie. He walked so damned quiet. Herbert always respected people who walked quiet. He turned back to the stand. Carter'd be back by to pay him. He'd wait.

Laura Lee was sleepy. She always got sleepy between twelve and two. It was then her day life reached out to claim her, the hours spent in the office dragged at her, and she wanted nothing so much as her own bed and the peace of sleep. About two-thirty she got her second wind and was all right. If she could last through the first spell of impossible weariness she was good for the rest of the night, for the kissing in the dark of the taxi and the early breakfast with the sun coming up. But she always had to get through the time when sleep claimed her. She'd developed a number of diversions to keep sleep away, because on weekends she didn't want to go home. When there was no work the next day she wanted to spend the night hours with Carter, living his life in the darkness, sleeping through the next day as he did. When she felt sleep coming she quit drinking, she got up and walked around, she tried to eat something, or smoke more, or talk. Tonight she'd almost given in to it, relaxing against Carter after laughing at Arlie's story, feeling her eyelids closing, smelling the peculiar smell of Carter and comfort. She stood up suddenly. "I'm going to sleep," she said.

"Go ahead," Carter said. "No law against it that I know of."

"No." She laughed, too loudly. "I don't want to go home yet."

"Didn't say, go home," Carter said mildly. "Sleep right where you were. I'll sit still."

She shook her head. "Let's get out and get some air."

"All right." Carter stood up. "Anybody want to ride around?" he said.

Julie shook her head. "We'll stay here."

Essie was half-asleep on the sofa herself. "If you see Dupree tell him where Estelle is," Julie said.

"O.K." Carter took Laura's hand. "Come on, sleepy," he said. "I'll wake you up."

Getting into the car they saw Herbert Winston waving at them from the corner. "Wants his damned money," Carter said. "I got to settle with Dupree before I turn it in." He waved and drove off. "Where you want to go, baby? You hungry?"

"Not yet. Besides, there's Blackjack standing in front of the café. I don't want to see him."

"O.K.," Carter said. He drove off the square. "How about a dip in the lake?"

"I don't know. Maybe."

He drove out the highway toward the lakefront. There's enough moon," he said.

"All right."

Laura was always reluctant to swim at night with Carter. She felt that it made her vulnerable to him. She thought that perhaps it was because she and Sonny used to slip off and go swimming at night. The lake had been forbidden to them but they'd go anyway, making a game of it, swimming in the moonlight off the old pier, then driving around and around the square in Sonny's old T-model to get her hair dry so Irene and J.O. wouldn't know where they'd been. Sonny always pretended it was because of her, but even then she'd known it wasn't. They didn't care about her. It was funny how she couldn't hate Sonny for having all the attention and love always. But she didn't. She guessed it was because home had seemed, if not pleasant, at least bearable when he had been there. So that she always thought of him as the normal thing in her life and the time of Sonny as a time when her family approached a normalcy, a calm placid existence like other people's. She knew this wasn't really true. Her home had never been a happy place, but she clung to the belief. Everybody has to think something.

The lake was black and silver in the moonlight. Carter turned down a gravel road to a clearing that widened into a beach. They got out of the car. There were small sounds and flutters in the trees around them, a host of night sounds magnified by the coming morning, whose smell already assaulted the upper air. "I'll go in," Carter said.

He took his pants and shirt off and waded out toward the deep water. She watched him for a few moments, then, frightened suddenly at having him so far out, pulled her dress and slip off and went into the water after him.

From the middle of the lake he watched her, standing white and small on the edge of the darkness, too far away to touch, too far away to speak to even, small and bright in the moonlight, Laura Lee. He turned and swam toward her, coming up beside her and smiling at her in the moonlight. "Wake you up?" he said.

She nodded. "It's cold," she said. "I don't see how it can be on a night like this, but it is."

"It's always cold under the surface," Carter said. He turned on his back and floated beside her, looking up at the area of sky washed by the moon. "She came up late tonight," he said.

"And bright."

"And cold."

"I don't think so," she said. "She looks warm and bright to me."

"Not to me," Carter said. "Cold, and white and bright and beautiful. But definitely cold."

Laura turned on her stomach and swam quickly away from him. He followed her. "I was talking about the moon," he said.

"Sure."

"You ready to get out?"

She didn't answer him, swimming back toward the beach, kicking a spray of water behind her. He followed her out and stood dripping on the rocky beach. She glanced at his wet knit shorts, then quickly picked up her clothes and went behind a tree. He stood there in his shorts looking after her. Then he sighed and put his pants and shirt back on over his wet underwear. "Come on out, honey," he said. "I'm decent."

She stepped around the tree toward him, her dress as neat and white as though she had just dressed for the evening, but her hair was wet, dripping onto her back. It made her seem strangely vulnerable to him. "Come kiss me," he said.

She turned her face up and he kissed her softly. He felt sad suddenly, soaked by water and moonlight and a malaise he couldn't name. "Let's go eat," he said.

On the way back to town she sat close beside him, holding his right hand against her while he drove slowly with his left. Occasionally she sighed a little, the sound smothered against him.

They passed the hospital and the bedspread plant and the grammar school. The traffic lights had been turned out and their blank eyes looked down on the lamplit intersections. Ahead of them the square loomed up blue and silent. Laura Lee sat up straight. "I'm wide awake now," she said.

"Did you see that fellow get off the train?" Carter said suddenly.

"Yes. I said so. Why?"

"I don't know. Wondered all of a sudden what he was

doing. Not many people come into town on the train any-more."

"Oh, some salesman."

"Maybe." He looked down at her hair, still clinging damply to her head. "You smell good," he said.

She frowned. "Please don't talk about it," she said.

Jackson Ferguson stood in front of the Majestic waiting for Dupree Harris to get back from the hospital. Behind him in the café Annie Brent waited on the owner of the poolhall and Herbert Winston. In front of him the square was empty. Occasionally a car passed through coming from Hunter City, the younger crowd coming in. The country club set had already gone in and the highway stretched blankly in the dark.

He leaned against the front of the café and remem-bered. It was funny how that glimpse of the man at the train had brought the time five years ago back to him. He tried to keep it underneath because he still felt it to be the prime cause of his precarious position on the force. He had to remember it enough to be forewarned by it, but he tried not to reconstruct the details. That was probably why he'd had trouble placing Julie Hobson, that deliberate repression of detail. And that was really all she'd been, a detail. Of course placing her didn't tell him what she was doing here now, but he wasn't ready to think of that yet. He knew he had to go through it all again, like plac-ing film in a projector, letting it run through its set of frames in his mind with the details this time. After that he'd face what Julie Hobson was doing in Bellefonte. And why the other one had got off the train.

Five years ago Ferguson had felt safe in his job. Belle-fonte had belonged to him with the certainty of long suzerainty. He had watched over it at that time for al-most twenty-five years.

It was a chilly evening in March when Jackson Fergu-son first came into Bellefonte. The town was much smaller then, made up of wooden stores clustered around the red-brick courthouse. It was in the early years of the depres-sion and it showed on the store fronts and the bleak side-walks. People moved slowly and dispiritedly. Even the soft air of spring didn't rouse them from a winter-long lethargy.

He stood on the edge of the square and yearned toward Bellefonte. He had spent his life so far in the fields and rows of tired cotton with town only a bauble hung in front of his eyes. Town, the place of mystery and maybe half a dozen trips a year when they would rattle along the road for most of the day in the wagon to stand on the pavements for a few hours and watch the store fronts behind which lurked other more intricate mysteries. He wasn't from Maynard County but it was the same, the courthouse and pavement and store fronts here looked exactly as they had in his own county seat. He did not examine why he had come to Bellefonte. He was running; from home, family, fields. But he was running from something else too and to escape it Bellefonte was really the wrong choice. Still, he had made it, unconsciously, telling himself dishonestly that his family wouldn't follow him here.

He owned a good pair of black pants and a frayed white shirt and a battered hat. His overalls he left behind. He spent the first night in an empty wagon bed behind Simms' Mule Barn.

In the morning the dawn came cold and he got up before daylight to wander back onto the square and watch it come to life. He was hungry but he had only a quarter in his pocket and he wasn't sure yet how he wanted to spend it.

The merchants came onto the square early, unlocking their doors and running out the awnings with an unwarranted optimism. He watched them, the drugstore owner, the drygoods store men, the grocers, all looking stooped and tired but determinedly cheerful in the early light. The square was gray, an indeterminate blur of buildings with none of last night's magic in them. He decided he didn't want to clerk in the stores.

The cafés looked more promising. Already there were smells of food and coffee in the air from the two on the square. He succumbed and went into one and ordered toast and coffee. But the interior of the café seemed dark and sad too. The grayness had come here and the smell of rancid grease and floor cleaner did little to dispel it. He went back onto the street.

As the day wore on he watched, seeing all the remembered magic of his youth fade irrevocably into the dingy streets of day. By noon he had drifted to the courthouse lawn to sit on the curbing and watch the old men playing checkers and the farmers lined along the curb with early produce. There was more life around the courthouse. Men went busily in and out of doors and drove away in Fords and trucks that still looked comparatively new. He watched them, musing on the ways of county and city government. He thought of the size a star gave a man.

The day warmed toward noon. He could feel himself sweating in his dark pants and long-sleeved shirt. At one o'clock he allowed himself a Coca-Cola. While he was drinking it, propped up against the side of the Sulphur Well just off the courthouse lawn, he became aware of a muted excitement. It was hard to pin it down, trace the center of emotion, but it was there. He could feel it raying out onto the quiet square. There was talk among the old men and among the farmers. Two or three of the merchants came out of their stores and stood looking toward the courthouse. By the time he had finished his Coca-Cola it had swelled to a muted roar.

A small man came out of the courthouse and stood on the steps, gesturing wildly. It was the telegraph operator from the station, but Ferguson didn't know that then. He only felt that for the first time since he'd come here this town had taken on the characteristics of a town, had moved to become the place of stir and excitement and mystery again.

The sheriff and two deputies had come onto the portico of the courthouse now. He moved toward them, drawn with the farmers and old men. Behind him he could hear the sound of footsteps hurrying across the square toward the courthouse. He stood still and listened.

The voices rose on the spring air, ripping into the stillness of southern afternoon: "Whole bunch of niggers done tried to kill some white boys . . ." "Telegraphed from the station up at Bridger's Junction . . ." "Got to take 'em off the train down at Red Creek."

He moved up again. They were going toward the cars and trucks parked around the courthouse now, and from indeterminate places shotguns had begun to appear. He moved surely and quickly around the milling farmers to the sheriff's side. "You better deputize some men," he said. "I'm willing to take a badge."

The sheriff turned and looked at him for a long measuring moment. "Get in the Ford over there with Wiley and Tom," he said finally.

They bounced along down a dusty road through the warm afternoon. From his place in the back seat he heard the sheriff's voice droning back to him and he pieced together the story. There had been some trouble in a gondola car of a freight train coming down out of Tennessee. Some boys had been thrown off the train and had gone back to Bridger's Junction to report it to the stationmaster. The stationmaster had wired ahead to the first stop but it had been too late to stop the train in Bellefonte. It had passed on to Red Creek and was being held there until someone could get in from the county seat. "Hope they ain't killed nobody," the sheriff said laconically. "You get these black bastards riled up they don't act like humans."

Jackson did not say anything. Beyond taking the badge he had no further thoughts for the present. He watched the country passing outside his window. He waited.

They could see the little crowd clustered around the general store before they pulled into the town. Red Creek was only a small station with a general store, and a gin, but most of the town seemed to be standing around the store. A tall man who appeared to be the storekeeper was trying to keep the crowd calmed down. The sheriff pulled off the road and they got out of the car. There were cars and trucks pulled up all around the crowd, and more coming down the road from Bellefonte. Jackson followed the sheriff's pushing shoulders through the crowd. They were standing together behind the tall man—a group of Negro boys and another of white ones. Jackson moved up and stood beside the sheriff.

"Get them into the truck," the sheriff said. Jackson went with the deputies. They roped the boys together and pushed them into the back of a truck, the white boys in one, the colored boys in another. Two of the boys looked smaller than the others and Jackson turned to look at them more closely. He saw that they weren't boys at all but girls got up in boys' clothes. It shocked him to see those girls coming off a freight train. In a dark and hidden way Jackson Ferguson was an extremely moral man. It was perhaps one of the reasons he was running. His morals

101

derived from brush-arbor meetings and a weekly Old Testament ranting by his father. They were not gentle morals. They were the perfect morals for a boy who wanted to become The Law.

He rode back to Bellefonte in the front of the truck that carried the Negro boys. At the jail he stood around, watching the milling deputies and the townspeople. There was a lot of yelling back and forth and running in and out of cell doors. He tried to hear what was going on but in the general confusion it was some time before he realized that the two girls had accused the Negro boys of rape and that the whole episode had changed character.

He had forgotten that he was hungry. As the day ended the early spring chill came into the air. He could smell the cooking from the sheriff's quarters and the close fetid smell of bodies. He went to the window and looked through the flat bars onto the square.

Night was coming. Below him stretching into the streets and across the lot from the jail was the beginning of the biggest crowd he had ever seen in his life. The new intelligence was just making its way through it and he could see it rise and flex and change, the whole crowd, not separate entities but one large massive moving protoplasm. He stared, fascinated. It swelled continually, fed from the outer edges by new arrivals. It made a noise now. The noise not separate, either, but a blended swell of sound, angry but muted. As dark came the sound grew too.

Ferguson watched. Behind him the business of the jail went on. There were steps and voices and yelling. Once the sheriff's wife came out and went into the cell and talked to the girls. The deputies leaned against the walls in the small hallway watching the frightened Negroes. They stood in their various attitudes around the cell, some defiant, some afraid, some only resigned. One of them, no more than thirteen, was crying, the sound moist and weary on the heavy air.

There were flashes of light from the crowd now, flashlights, lanterns, here and there a few primitive torches. The sheriff touched his shoulder. "You armed?" he said.

Jackson shook his head and the sheriff handed him a pistol and went back to his room at the end of the hallway.

Jackson watched. There were single entities breaking

out of the crowd now, haranguing the rest of them, holding up ropes and whooping over the roar. The crowd grew. He turned and went back to the deputies who still stood leaning against the wall. "Why don't we take these boys out of here and get them to the big jail over at Gatesburg?" he said.

The deputies pushed away from the wall and looked at him. They were sweating, the shine of it on their faces. "What you talking about?" Wiley said.

"We can't hold this little ole crackerbox of a jail," Jackson said.

"We can't get 'em through that crowd down there neither," Tom said.

"We got guns. We got blackjacks," Jackson said. "We can get 'em through. It might take some doing. But I bet I can do it."

They looked at him uncertainly. They hadn't gauged the sheriff yet. They didn't know what he wanted them to do and they were scared. This man didn't seem to be afraid. "You been watching that crowd?" Wiley said.

Jackson nodded. "We can get 'em through and to the truck. Can you open the cell?"

They moved in front of him, carried on by the authority that had come into his voice. Wiley opened the door. The Negroes cringed into the corners. Some of them put their hands over their faces and one old man put the boy gently behind him. Two of them did not step back at all. They walked forward and stood waiting, wary but unafraid. Wiley took handcuffs and started linking them together in pairs.

The door opened and the sheriff walked into the cell. He looked around carefully. "What the hell do you think you're doing?" he said.

"We figured to get these boys over to a bigger jail, Gatesburg or somewhere," Wiley said.

"Are you crazy?" the sheriff said. He looked agitated and his voice had a ragged sound. "You can't take those boys out there. They'd have them away from you in two minutes."

Jackson moved back and stood watching them. The sheriff turned toward him, watching his face. "You got better sense than that, haven't you?" he said. "You look like you have."

"But he . . ." Wiley began.

Jackson spoke quickly. "Maybe you're right, sheriff," he said. "A crowd can be mighty hard to judge." He looked at the other deputies. They looked back warily but they didn't say anything. They were country boys who had never worked for anyone but the sheriff and they were used to authority, and to the capriciousness of that authority. Already they were accepting Ferguson as one of the leaders. They waited.

"You reckon we're gonna be able to hold this jail though?" Jackson said.

"We're gonna have to till I can get the State Guard here," the sheriff said. "This has done gone too far to do nothing about. Them two girls is sticking to their story and that story's out on that square right now. I figure the Guard'll get here by maybe four, five in the morning. We just got to hold her till then."

Jackson went back to the window. Behind him he could hear Wiley and Tom muttering, but he didn't turn toward them. He'd had an idea but it hadn't worked out. It had been only half formed anyway. Watching that crowd, he had known that whichever way it had gone, whether they had gotten the Negroes through and into the trucks or whether the crowd had taken them, as an offering from them, he would have been somebody, something. He would at least have had a job. But it hadn't worked. He had misjudged the sheriff. So he changed plans, quickly and with no regret. It didn't matter which way he got what he was after. In some towns the sheriff was strong, in others he was not. He'd misjudged this one, but he wouldn't again. He moved forward to the window. A circle of cars had drawn up now around the edges of the crowd and the headlights had been turned on, throwing slashes of light through the upturned faces.

He walked back down the short hall to the room where the sheriff sat at his desk, a shotgun across his lap. "Sheriff," he said. "I was thinking. Surely there's some men here in this town. Businessmen. Folks like that could come down and help us out. Don't you reckon?"

David Hall looked up at him. "By God, boy, you're right," he said. "I'll just make a few calls."

At four o'clock when the State Guard pulled into Belle-fonte, walking swiftly and sure-footedly through the crowd, to take the Negroes with them to Gatesburg, the leading citizens of the town were standing casually in front of the jail, rifles and shotguns across their arms. They were talking crops and weather and depression, but they were standing between the crowd and the jail door. Sheriff Hall was standing in the hallway waiting to open the cell to the Guard, and Jackson Ferguson, in the cold light of a cold spring morning, was Bellefonte's newest deputy.

He moved restlessly, the remembering making him tired suddenly. It use to be that remembering that crowd and the sound of it on the air had made him restless, filled him with a sort of unidentified excitement. But he was getting older. Now it only seemed like something that had happened a long time ago. The crowd as he remembered them had become old-fashiond snapshots, outdated and outworn, the country boy in the black pants with the empty stomach seemed a stranger to him. He had come too far since that night.

Through the years he had moved from the sheriff's office, raiding stills at first, jostling over the rutted country roads with an ax beside him on the front seat. Later when the bootlegging became centralized he had refused to collect the payoff and had moved into town. As the town grew and the people of Bellefonte learned to live at night, he had gradually shifted his ground to the night side, asking for and getting the patrol job that had long been his objective. To live in the dark, when the streets were his alone, when those who were out had to take him into account. It had been a good time for a good number of years. The changes had come into the town, but they did not touch him. They were mostly changes of the day, and the day didn't interest him. He had long ago made himself indispensable to Sheriff Hall and therefore to his successors. He did not want to be sheriff himself. It had never occurred to him. Being sheriff asked too much of him. For one thing he would have to stand election. The thought of a campaign in the bright hot light of day, and the handshaking and picnic speeches, filled him with horror. He had what he wanted. Or had had. Until five years ago, when he had made his first mistake.

He looked up. Dupree Harris had driven onto the

square and parked in front of the café. "Well?" Ferguson said as he came toward him.

"I don't know." Dupree said. "Dr. Kent's out there with him. You seen Carter McCain around here?"

Ferguson shook his head. "Herbert Winston's in there." He nodded toward the café. "Maybe he's seen him."

"Coffee?" Dupree said.

Jackson shook his head. "Better get back around," he said. "I been standing here a pretty long time."

He walked off, pacing his way carefully, looking into the empty stores. Dupree shook his head and went into the café. "You see Carter?" he said to Herbert Winston.

"Too late to catch," Herbert said.

The store fronts loomed against the sidewalks, the single bulbs in the rear of the stores throwing into relief the deserted counters. At the bank the light over the night-deposit slot softened the granite around it, giving the cold stone a demilife among the shadows. In front of the picture show the smell of popcorn lingered on the predawn air. Ferguson watched the doors, trying the night latches, looking into the gloom of the closed markets, matching his footsteps to the change of pavement where the sidewalks sloped or cracked. Silence. He listened to his own footsteps move through it, pausing here and there to test the pause. They were gone now, the entities who pushed and whirled and moved through the early evening, the voices and shuffling feet, the shouts and laughter. Those entities he remembered as becoming one. It was this that he had learned on the first night of his deputyship, this that held him thrall to these people, as well as giving him his power over them. Their ability to move and meet and meld, to cease to be entities, becoming, through one word, one connotation, a single strong certain headless body with the power to move and speak and do, from one indeterminate center with a million coordinated legs and arms, the bidding of that indeterminate force.

They were gone now, dispersed, lying separately and alone in their numberless beds, individual, dreaming. But he knew what they could be subtracted into, how the individuality could be submerged in darkness. He walked alone in the empty square of night, remembering.

It had been on Halloween. Late October, when the days were cold at morning and hot at midday, when the sun went down red and suddenly and the winds blew night into the edge of winter. He came out early because before dark on this night it would begin, the smaller children in their eyeholed sheets running across streets like the actuality of which they were imitation, causing cars to swerve and brake in the halflight. When full dark came there would be the teen-agers, hiding in alleys and behind garages, ready to carry lawn furniture into the treetops or smear paint across the bricks of the high school. In recent years they had told him to ignore anything that looked as though it might be going to happen off the square. He was to stay within its perimeters and watch the stores. They had long ago given up on the soaping of windows, but he could try to stop paint. He could ignore the displacement of signs and garbage cans but he must try to stop actual theft. He knew the limits. He had watched them for many years now. He could tell within seconds when the intent was more than mischief. He could spot trouble from the other side of the square. He never did much about it beyond bringing his presence onto the scene. It was enough. He was scornful of all of Halloween. He knew it for what it was, the remnant of the bacchanalia, the hope that one night a year of sanctioned destruction would deter them for 364 days. And he knew that it didn't work. The ones whom they had cause to fear purged nothing on Halloween, they scorned it, giving a reluctant service to it by a few mean acts, waiting through it until a time of dark again. It was the ones who never did anything or wanted to who came out on Halloween; the timid and careless, the healthy normal kids of day who participated in destruction only because it was expected of them. It purged nothing, because those who participated had nothing to purge.

Trick-or-treat was late in coming to Alabama, that businessman's notion of Halloween manipulated to trick adults into the buying of candy and orange-and-black sacks. For the younger children the parade was still the thing. Dressing up to walk up and down the lighted streets, peering out from behind the close-fitting, cloth-smelling masks onto a world made strange, throwing confetti and beating on tambourines. He had learned to ignore this too, stepping carefully around the small bright ghosts that stalked the streets, not caring yet which of them would become

107

the hunted of tomorrow. Time enough for that. Now they were only noise. They hadn't learned the connotations that would make them more or less.

He knew what the parents expected of him, the studied indifference he should assume while the crowds lasted. He didn't give it to them. He walked his normal round, kept his perimeters. He was contemptuous of them all because he knew nothing would actually happen. The rites had worn too thin. There would be no catharsis, no melding of purpose. He had seen that happen once and he knew it did not happen from plan, not any more. Perhaps there had been a time in the far past when man had called up by will the shadow side to perform on command for him, but not now. It was gradually being covered by the layers of civilization. Only something strong and sudden and not-understood could bring it forth to command and move a faceless mindless mass again.

At ten o'clock, while standing on the corner waiting for the light to change, a crowd of high school girls had swept by him and doused him with cheap perfume from the ten-cent store. He ignored that, too, knowing with the beginnings of contemptuous rage that he must walk for the rest of the night smelling of whorehouse, wondering briefly what sort of mind had thought of that one. It was almost worthy, at least an idea in the midst of formless milling. If he could have found a smile inside him he might have smiled.

At ten-thirty he was on the dark side of the square, the south side away from the drugstores and picture shows. It was quiet here, comparatively. There was nothing open to attract a crowd. A few children made the whole circuit, but not many. By ten-thirty even these hardy ones were confining themselves to the north and west. He took his usual amount of time here, careful to look into the small alley that ran between the hardware store and the dress shop, stopping at the corner to look into the fire station and the dark steps that led to the second story of the City Hall. As he passed the lighted window of the locker plant, noting the time on the electric clock, he felt trouble come onto the north side of the square. He could not have said how he felt it; certainly there was nothing to hear above the noises of chaos, certainly there was nothing to see but the empty street in front of him. But he knew. He didn't change his route, he didn't cut across the square. He continued walking down the south side, across the street and back across, up the deserted east side, looking carefully into the soap-smeared glass fronts of the car agencies, checking the east-side stores, crossing again at the corner, and again, and so down the north side to the northwest corner.

The crowd was already beginning to gather. He could see it from up the block but he didn't hurry, moving calmly and purposefully along his regular route. As he came up to the corner those in the back of the crowd saw him and began to move sideways, opening the lane through which he walked without acknowledging any of them. He put his hand on his blackjack and walked through to the front of the crowd.

There was a Negro man standing in a clear space in the center of the crowd. He was dressed in a gray pin-striped suit and he wore a snap-brim hat. Ferguson saw immediately that the suit had cost twice as much as any suit he had ever owned. The shoes were cordovan leather, polished, but not to too high a gloss, neat elegant shoes of expensive leather. Impossible shoes for a Negro man on the corner of North Street in Bellefonte, Alabama. His eye registered all this in one quick dart. It also registered the crowd of hecklers around the Negro, the poolroom rowdies, the ragtail element of the high school, the older boys of Beat 4 in their Sunday clothes, put on carefully for a night in town.

He scanned their faces, the surprise coming up in him as he felt his mind struggling to hold it back. He recognized what he saw on those faces and he had to admit that he hadn't expected to see it, hadn't believed it existed, had spent years ignoring the possibility of it on a Halloween night. He took the blackjack out of its thongs.

They did not see him at first, caught in the glare of the corner street light, involved in the baiting, watching the Negro, they didn't look toward the edge of the crowd. It was a mixed crowd, composed of mothers and costumed children, of high-school students, of the holidaymakers in masks and caps and small brass bells. But watching those few faces in the center Jackson Ferguson knew the components meant nothing. It was a crowd, capable of becoming something else instantaneously, suddenly, over-whelmingly. He smelled it.

The leader was a tall muscled boy from Holly Springs. Ferguson had had some trouble with him before on Saturday nights. He stood out from the circle of his cronies, pointing one dirty-nailed finger at the Negro, laughing loudly. "What are you got up to be?" he was saying. "A white man? Is that what you're got up to be for Halloween?"

The circle moved, converging in.

"I Mr. Sonny's nigger," the man said softly. "I done come here with Mr. Sonny. You better move back, white folks, and let me get on to his car. I got to drive him somewheres."

Ferguson listened, astonished to hear the unmistakable accents of Alabama in the Negro's voice. He hadn't expected it. The Negroes stayed away from the square on Halloween just as they did at election and during court session. Because of his presence here on the masked and costumed corner, because of the shoes and the clothes, Ferguson had expected the accents of the North. He had been waiting for the snappy answer, the reference to authority, the masked sneer. When it did not come there was a hesitation in his mind. The trained precision of what to do did not follow. This was a local Negro. He looked under the hatbrim, trying to recognize the face. It was vaguely familiar but no name came with the recognition, neither for the Negro nor of the white family for which he might have worked. So he couldn't be sure. He was puzzled and he held back, not moving, while the white boy reached out one broganed foot and tripped the Negro as he started to push through the crowd.

The Negro sprawled face down on the pavement. His hat had rolled off and was being kicked into the street by two of the boys. He did not move, lying still, immobile in the circled light of the lamppost—waiting.

Ferguson had brought the blackjack up and behind him and down for the second time before he realized what he was doing. There had been no thought before the action; nothing. He had stepped forward and the blackjack was now in front of him, in contact with the black head. He watched it rising and falling in a bemused wonder, seeing his hand go up and out of sight and come down, the muscles in his back stretched to meet the command, given from somewhere not the forefront of his mind.

There was no sound on the corner. They stood quiet, watching him. Occasionally there would be a sharp rattle of tambourine, silenced suddenly by an adult hand. The blackjack rose and fell in a sort of rhythm. Later he was to remember the look on the faces around him changing, the edging back and away, and the sound somewhere in the dark beyond the lamp of someone being sick.

He never understood fully what stopped him, any more than what had actually possessed him, laying open his mind like a sharp knife stroke to allow the dark ooze beneath up and into light. He stopped suddenly, as unthoughtedly as he had begun, and leaning forward he put his hand into the collar of the pin-striped suit and dragged the black and frightening force behind him, limp and unconscious and unthreatening now, toward the red-brick jail. The one clear thought that came to him was, Me too. Of course. It's in me too. It was a long time later before the implications had come to him, the feeling of taking upon himself in that dark hour the needs and desires and dark mindless deeds of all of them. Only later did he see himself in the role of savior, taking upon himself by his own sudden deed the sins of the town he walked for. It gave him an added hold over them, an added debt to them. It was all the more reason why he could not leave his perimeters to someone else.

The jailer had been sitting on a splint-bottomed chair propped against the side of the building, reading a dime western. "What you got there, Mr. Ferguson?" he said mildly, standing up and handing the keys toward him.

He didn't answer, going down the urine-reeking corridor to the remembered cell door, opening it and dumping the body inside with a steady, uninterested hand. He did not even look back, giving the keys to the jailer in one firm movement and going on out the front of the jail. At the street he turned back. "You better get Doc to look at him," he said. Five minutes later he was walking again up the south side of the square.

It was eleven-forty-five when they came after him, the sheriff walking quickly onto the square by the courthouse and watching until he saw him waiting for the light at the north corner. He called across the square, his voice carrying above the scattered sounds still riding the air of mid-night. "Ferguson," he said. "Get over here."

He waited for the light and crossed over, cutting across the square by the Sulphur Well. The sheriff stood slouched comfortably against a car on the edge of the courthouse lawn. Behind him was Thurston Marlow, the other night deputy. "You was a little heavyhanded on that nigger, wasn't you?" Sheriff Wright said.

"He was causing trouble," Ferguson said.

"I didn't say he wasn't," Wright said. "I says you were a mite heavyhanded."

"He's alive, ain't he?" Ferguson said.

Wright watched him, his eyes narrowing in the light from the lamppost. "Would you be surprised if he wasn't?" he said.

"Yes," Ferguson said. "Yes, I would. I didn't kill that bastard. I know when I quit."

"All right," Wright said. "All right about that. He is alive. But I got something to tell you, Ferguson, and you better listen. That nigger belongs to that Colvin boy. He's been with them Colvins ever since he was born. His grandfolks was born into slavery in a shack on what used to be the Colvin cotton place up the cove. He weren't no yankee nigger, though I admit he was got up like one. He was one of the big folks'. You just made yourself a little mistake. I tell you now, because Sonny Colvin is setting over yonder at that jail right now waiting to swear out a complaint against you and I don't know whether you're worth me saving."

Ferguson watched him. He didn't glance toward Thurston Marlow but he was aware of him, standing in proper deference just behind the sheriff and a little to one side. He needed to summon up rage or outrage—any emotion—but it wasn't in him. He felt as cleansed of all emotion as if a wind had ripped through him. Cleaned and swept and free for the first time since he'd stood in that barred window and watched something he didn't understand.

"I been walking for this town for a pretty long time now," he said.

"Yes," Wright said. "And I ain't saying you ain't useful. You've always made yourself useful. But times ain't like they used to be, Jackson. The city bunch are trying to run more and more of our business. You know that, if you've taken the trouble to look anywhere besides the pavement in front of you for the last four years. It's creeping up on us. They're already talking about putting the town deputies under a town jurisdiction. And you know who runs this town. Do you reckon you can make yourself useful enough to any of them Wallaces? Do you reckon you can beat out one of their hand-picked boys for your own job?"

Ferguson still didn't answer him, watching both him and Thurston now, seeing one small flicker in Thurston's eye that could mean anything.

He knew the sheriff was talking fact. He had seen the Wallaces moving up through the years, watched them taking the town simply and plainly. But he hadn't mended his fences enough in that direction. He hadn't because he'd had a blind spot. He'd assumed they wanted the town and that they were happy to see the county run by the county officials. He'd given them credit for knowing when things were run to everybody's advantage. What he hadn't counted on was that eventually they'd have to turn that advantage. The time would come when they would want to take all non-Wallace fingers out of the pie.

"What do you want?" he said.

"I just like to know who's on my side," Wright said.

"All right," Jackson said. "I reckon that's fair enough."

"Well?" Wright said again.

"I never lost nothing around the Wallaces," Ferguson said.

"Come on then." Wright turned without looking at him again and led the way across the courthouse lawn. Thurston Marlow stayed on the square, watching lazily the few last revelers waiting for midnight.

He did not know how it had been accomplished, where and when and how much money had changed hands. The sheriff didn't want him to know. He did know that by morning Sonny Colvin and the nigger were out of Belle-fonte and that he began the long bleak nights of November on his regular patrol. It was never the same though. He felt the difference rising up from the cold pavements. From the corners he watched Thurston Marlow driving in the new city car around town, usurping with mechanization first the outlying areas, then the train station, and later more and more often the car would be parked near the taxi stand or the filling stations, creeping steadily into his province of night. When Sheriff Wright retired, his successor followed the line laid down in the distant past by some long-forgotten county party, but the changes were beginning. By that time there was a Wallace in the mayor's chair.

It was time for coffee again. Ferguson reached the café and went inside, blinking in the glare of light. Dupree set the cup before him automatically and he drank from it the same way, looking through his steel-rimmed spectacles at the bright cans of soup stacked behind the counter, letting his mind run on in its prearranged groove, unrolling the film to the time where Julie Hobson would appear, whole, intact, in place.

Twice a year Ferguson made a trip to Chattanooga. He took a weekend off once in early June and again just before Christmas. He would put on a black coat and white shirt and a black string tie, all still smelling faintly of mothballs, and catch the morning train. Once in the city he went to a chain cafeteria on the main street and treated himself to a shrimp cocktail and a hot roast beef sandwich with potatoes, and a slice of cherry pie. The menu never varied. That afternoon he would treat himself to the current movie at the Tivoli Theater, watching with impartial interest whatever appeared on the screen. The movie itself did not really matter to him. The same movie would play in Bellefonte within a few months. It was the theater he liked, the huge dim blue-lighted cave with the niches along the walls filled with vases of ever-blooming wax roses, the long strips of red carpet in the aisles, the silver curtain over which played the red, blue, and green lights of promise. And most of all the high blue ceiling, dotted with pinpoints of light like a special corner of the universe in which the stars were fixed, immovable, and stripped of their power to awe or frighten.

After the movie he would walk up the busy main street of the town, noting the crowds and the smell of popcorn and baking sweet rolls. He would come to the bakery and treat himself to a sack of fresh-made doughnuts. These he would take to a small restaurant on a side street and, ordering a pot of coffee, consume them slowly and thoughtfully in the early night.

He would take a taxi then to the remote corner of town

114

where the brothel he had attended for twenty years was located. He spent the night there, being by this time possessed of a sort of squatter's right for the twice-yearly trips. He would sleep late, rising to walk to a small café on the corner, where he breakfasted slowly in the early afternoon light. Then he called another taxi and caught the afternoon train back to Bellefonte.

His schedule had not changed in all the twenty years. There had never been any reason for change, chance had never lured him into a different pattern, another street, another restaurant or theater or brothel. His route was as prearranged as that of Halley's Comet. Until the Christmas after the incident of Halloween.

Sitting in the cafeteria on that December day, watching the Christmas crowds milling outside the plate-glass window, savoring the last of the cherry pie and coffee, he had thought, I'm getting on. It's not quite the fun it used to be. But later, in the dim cave of the theater, he had forgotten that and when he took the taxi to the familiar address he felt no different than he did every December of every year. He did not really anticipate the trip so much as he felt a satisfaction in the accomplishment of it. The evening ending to a holiday. He got out on the familiar corner and paid the taxi driver. He didn't tip him. He never did.

The car was parked in front of the brick building. He didn't think anything about it, noticing it as he did everything in his field of vision, seeing that it was a Cadillac and that it had a local tag with a small number. He walked on by it and already had his foot on the bottom step when the voice spoke. "Come on over here," it said.

He hesitated, then went on, placing his other foot on the second step. The headlights switched on then and the voice came again. "Mr. Ferguson," it said out of the darkness. "Come on over here."

Still he went on, placing his right foot on the third step. The voice spoke again. "There's a forty-five trained on your back," it said softly.

He turned, coming back down the steps as slowly as he had gone up them, crossing to the curb with no haste. He could see the face in the window now under the dark hat, above the white scarf. The thought that came to him then and stayed with him through the rest of it was simple: *This is just like the picture show.* "Get in," the man said.

He walked around the car, feeling his hand going automatically to the place where the blackjack should be and not finding it. He had the gun in his inside holster but it wasn't plausible to reach for it. Not now. He got into the car.

"Where are we going?" he said once as they pulled into the street.

"A friend of mine's got some business with you," the man said.

They didn't speak again, sitting beside each other like statues until the car pulled into the parking lot behind the town's best hotel. He thought then of breaking and running for it, but the man was out of the car standing beside him, holding his hand negligently in his pocket, joking with the parking lot attendant, so that he thought, They aren't going to kill me because he wouldn't bring me here to talk to that guy first.

They went around and up in the service elevator and along a carpeted corridor and into a room.

He knew, just looking around, that it was the best suite in the hotel, even though he'd never been in the best suite of any hotel. The man with him, the same thin-faced tall man he'd seen get off the midnight train in Bellefonte just tonight, closed the door behind them and slid the bolt.

He recognized the figure sitting in the chair across the room. He'd watched him grow up in Bellefonte, seen him driving a battered T-model around the square, his sister beside him, seen him on Saturday nights standing in front of the drugstore with the high-school kids. He hadn't seen him in several years now, but he knew him. Or thought he did. There was a difference in him that made him uncertain, even though he knew who he was. It had to be him because there was nobody else who, having any unfinished business with him, would take the trouble of catching him in Chattanooga to transact it. What gave him the uncertainty was that he couldn't place the high school boy he knew in this unreal picture-show setting. It didn't make any sense.

Sonny Colvin watched him. Ferguson stood still in front of Sonny and watched him too. When he didn't look away Sonny raised one hand and snapped his fingers. The door opened and the Negro of Halloween night came into the room. He looked all right to Ferguson. He figured they'd

116

patched him up O.K. The Negro didn't say anything either. He just stood there, watching him too, his eyes blank.

"You got anything to say?" Sonny said suddenly.

Ferguson shook his head.

"Just like that," Sonny said. "Nothing. You beat a man half to death and as near as I can figger it don't even get reprimanded for it and you ain't got nothing to say."

He snapped his fingers again and a Negro woman came into the room carrying a tray with a bottle and soda and glasses on it. She set it down and went back out of the room.

Sonny poured himself a drink and sat back in the chair. "You know any reason why I shouldn't put the fear of God into you?" he said, smiling now.

Ferguson spoke then. He looked around at the whole unbelievable charade and spoke. "I'm The Law," he said firmly. "I do what I do to keep the peace. Who are you?"

Sonny's eyes flickered. "Tell him, Bagley," he said.

The tall man snickered, a low whinnying sound. "You ever hear of Sherman Green?" he said.

Ferguson turned toward him. "Well, I don't reckon there's anybody that hasn't heard of him," he said slowly. "Even us simple folk from Bellefonte know who runs the east coast part of the combine. But I know one thing for sure. That ain't him. That's Sonny Colvin that grew up right in Bellefonte himself."

"Yeah," the man said. "But Sonny here's sort of an important fellow to Green."

"Is that right?" Ferguson said. He looked straight ahead of him at the flowered draperies on the windows. He wasn't going to give them the satisfaction of knowing anything they said could make an impression on him.

Sonny snapped his fingers again and the Negro handed him a fresh drink. "You like being The Law, don't you?" he said.

Ferguson didn't answer him.

"Maybe we'll change your mind about that," Sonny said. He nodded at the tall man, who nodded at Ferguson in turn, and they went out the door.

Going down the long hotel corridor, walking slowly on the bright red carpet roses, he thought of running, but he knew he wouldn't. He thought too of trying to do some-

117

thing in the elevator, but he knew he wouldn't do that either. Because by now he was beginning to believe the thing that left him cold with rage and chagrin and a firm determination *not* to do anything. *They were having him on.* He didn't know why he thought this or how he knew it. It was a feeling only, the sort of instinct that could make him spot a half-formed shadow in a doorway half a block away. Certainly this man was armed, and just as certainly he wouldn't hesitate to use a gun. No doubt he had used it—and well. That was his obvious function. Ferguson didn't need the picture shows to tell him Bagley was a trigger. He knew that too with the same dark instinct. But he wasn't going to use that gun on Jackson Ferguson. And the reason was very simple. He wasn't worth it. Going down that corridor, looking ahead stolidly toward the elevators, he kept thinking wryly, *Not worth the powder to shoot him with.* And the grim flash of humor only increased his rage and his determination to show nothing.

They reached the elevator just as the doors slid open. A girl got out. She was wearing a fur coat and a small black hat tilted on one side of her head. She looked him full in the face and then turned toward Bagley, a faint smile tucking the corner of her mouth. She walked on down the hall and they got into the elevator.

Ferguson didn't speak to Bagley again. Not once during the ride into the country, the long slow ride during which the taunts and jeers and threats sounded around him in the closed car, the ride during which not once was a hand laid on him, only the voice, whipping him with its laughter and cold hate. Then miles out of town Bagley stopped the car. He reached across him and opened the door and pushed him out onto the side of the dusty dirt road.

He got up and dusted himself off. The taillights had already disappeared into the distance. He walked back along the road until he came to a filling station where he called into town and got a taxi. He went back to the brothel and spent the rest of the night and caught the morning train home to Bellefonte. Only he never made his biannual trip to Chattanooga again. He never wanted to.

And tonight, seeing Bagley get off that train and saunter easily and casually down the gravel toward the corner, the indignation had overwhelmed him. If it had not been for the instant's flash of recognition of Julie Hobson, his mind seeing her get off that elevator, her mouth tucked into that half-smile, he might have acted. But that stopped him. And luckily. For the rage was too instant and too complete to allow for planning, and he needed the time for that. It was not that Julie Hobson had spent the whole summer sitting in his town while he wondered who she was, not that he had been made a fool of. It was the amusement, the arrogance and sheer contempt that Sonny Colvin must have toward him to allow Bagley to walk into that town at midnight as casually as a shoe salesman.

He stopped on the edge of the square and looked up toward Arlie Machen's garage apartment where lights in the living room proclaimed the occupants still up and about in the night. Then he walked over and tested the latch on the door of the corner drygoods store.

3.

"I'LL go with you," Laura Lee said when Dupree told them about Jake.

Carter shook his head. "I'd rather you didn't," he said.

"But I want to."

He shook his head again, watching her white face under the bright fluorescence of the café lights. "Go back down to Arlie's. I'll come for you."

There was a wary look in her eyes and he pulled her away from the counter to one of the booths. "Look, honey," he said. "For all I know the old guy's dying. The whole damned family'll probably end up out there taking on like they do when something like this happens. I'd rather have you safe with Julie while I look into it. Please. For me."

She watched him, not answering. "I don't want to be without you," she said. "I'm afraid. I don't want to go home."

"I didn't say, go home," Carter said patiently. "I said go back with Arlie and Julie. I'll come for you." Then, seeing the hesitancy still on her face, he firmed his voice. "Come on," he said. "It's either that or go home. I'm not going to drag you out to that damned hospital in the middle of the night."

She got up and followed him out of the café and down the street to Arlie's. She stood just inside the door while he talked to Arlie and Julie, and watched silently while he went across the hall to Jake's rented room to see if there was anything he could take out to him. When he turned to her to kiss her she jerked away from him. He shrugged and went on down the steps. She stood with her face pressed against the window, watching him gun the motor and disappear around the corner toward the south.

She didn't know why she felt the way she did. She never knew. Common sense told her she had been betrayed. Common sense told her he was taking care of her. But the part of Laura Lee that made her life the worrisome thing it was felt betrayed, felt shoved aside, left out, forgotten. She pressed her face against the window glass and cried.

Carter drove through the late night toward the hospital. He was worried about Jake and worried about Laura Lee. He took the corner into the hospital lot too quickly, cursing himself briefly as he pulled up in the parking space around the emergency entrance.

He went up the steps quickly, looking into the brightly lit reception room, seeing the empty desk and wondering where the night nurse was. He passed through the archway and into the hall, looking for Will. He didn't see him either. The blue corridor lights made him uneasy and he paused, looking down the length of dead space bisecting the rows of rooms that housed the sick and dying. He started to take out a cigarette, then put the pack back in his pocket. He cleared his throat but no one responded to him and he went on down the corridor, looking at the blank faces of shut doors and the black spaces where some of them had been left open. Someone murmured in his sleep, a small sad sound in silence. He shook his head and stopped again.

A door opened down the hall and Dr. Kent came out. He walked toward him, noding back toward the entrance room. Carter turned and followed him. The doctor sat down on the edge of the desk and lit a cigarette. Carter lit one too. Dr. Kent looked around the room in annoyance. "Where the hell's Betty?" he said. Then shrugged. "McCain?" he said to Carter.

"That's right," Carter said. "He's my uncle."

"Well." Dr. Kent pulled one knee up and clasped it between his hands. He talked around the cigarette with short harsh syllables. "Heart. So I can't really tell. But I can't give him too much chance. He's old and he's pretty far gone on alcohol. Still, he might pull through tomorrow and be throwing a binge in a month. I wouldn't say one way or the other. But if not this time, the next one. Sure. And if he keeps on drinking like he is it won't be long till the next one. I've talked to him and I don't figure he's going to quit drinking. He's pretty decided about that. I'd say he knows his own chances and has for a long time, and that he likes it this way, and this is the way he wants to go. If we can keep him quiet enough and still enough and sober enough he may pull through this one. And he may be gone by morning, too. You can't really say." He put his cigarette out in the ashtray.

"Can I see him?" Carter said.

"Sure. He's about half under sedation, but conscious. Just don't stay long or let him talk too much." He looked around the room again. "You see the night nurse?" he said.

Carter shook his head. "She wasn't here when I came in."

Dr. Kent cursed briefly. "I'll look in on him in the morning," he said. "If you see Miss Dawson will you tell her I'm on my way out to the lake?"

"Sure," Carter said. "I'll tell her. Thanks, doc." He went back down the dimly lit corridor to the room he'd seen the doctor come out of.

Betty Dawson and Will McCain were making love on a hospital bed in a room just off the corridor, within range of the telephone bell and the buzzer on Betty's desk. They heard Carter come in and Betty raised up, but Will pushed her back down on the pillow. "It's Carter," he said. "I know the way the son-of-a-bitch drives up. He'll find him."

Betty lay still, listening to Dr. Kent come into the hall and go into the reception room with Carter. She heard him ask about her and she smiled in the dark.

She had come in here with Will with no thought about it at all. If she had taken time to think about it she wouldn't have done it, of course. He'd reached out and touched her and she'd thought instantly the one word, Yes. "Where?" he said, and she'd led the way into the empty room.

He was young and awkward and completely without finesse, but these very things excited her. She was used to the practiced love-making of Dr. Kent and the very suddenness, urgency, and awkward violence of this act made her react more violently than she ever had.

She reached up now, while Dr. Kent was still outside, and drew Will back down beside her. "O.K., baby," he said in her ear. "I'm as ready as you are. In fact, we can stay here all night for all of me."

"I'll have to get back out there," she murmured. "The floor nurse . . ."

"Sure," Will said. "In a minute."

But it was Will who got up first. He went to the door and looked out onto the lighted corridor. "I better get down yonder and see about Carter," he said.

"You want to see me again?" Betty said.

"Sure, baby," Will said. "When's your night off?"

For a moment, in the darkness, she had an impulse to tell him to go away. It was the same impulse she'd had the first time she'd been with Dr. Kent. Something from her old Baptist upbringing telling her to get off the road to hell and be a good girl and repent before it was too late. But it was already too late. That was the nasty thing about it. You only had the one chance. You only had one cherry. Just one, and after it was gone what the hell difference did it make? You couldn't bring it back, no matter how goody-goody for the rest of time you were. So she sighed and said, "Tomorrow night."

"I'll see you, baby. Eight, huh? Maybe I can dig up some beer." He went out and shut the door.

She got up and pulled at her wrinkled uniform and went into the bathroom. Her face stared back at her from the mirror over the wash basin. "I hate you, you bitch," she told it quietly. "I hate you because you look just the way you always have."

Will walked down the corridor toward his Uncle Jake's room, grinning to himself. He felt good. He guessed he felt better than he ever had in his life. That was the way the ball bounced. You'd feel about as low and miserable as possible and then something like this would just drop right into your lap. It just went to show that bastards like Carter and Arlie with their damned steady girls weren't so all-fired well-fixed as they thought. Because women were completely unpredictable. Nobody could have told him a half hour ago that he would lay Betty Dawson. He hardly knew her. And God knew he hadn't even had to try. He'd just put out one hand and there she was. Just like that. It made you wonder. It made you wonder about the reality of anything. But he wasn't going to start that again. Thinking never got you anywhere. You just had to take what came and like it and to hell with the rest.

He stopped outside the door to Jake's room. He could hear Carter's voice, then Jake's, low and hesitant. Something about the sound made him stop outside the door without going in. He leaned against the wall and put his ear against the door and waited.

"I guess they told you not to let me talk," Jake was saying. "Damned nonsense. It's the only thing I been doing for sixty years and I don't figure to stop now."

Carter drew a chair up by the bed and took out a cigarette, holding it uneasily without lighting it.

"Go on and smoke, boy," Jake said. "God knows a little more tobacco smoke ain't gonna tip any scales one way or the other." He laughed softly. "What's the matter with that young Dr. Kent?" he said. "He acts like a man with a problem. Hurry. Hurry. Hurry. Slow down a little he'll live longer."

"Hadn't you better rest?" Carter said.

"No. I reckon not. I'm gonna have a long enough time for that. Got a few things I want to tell you first too, by God." He moved his head on the white pillow. "You in love with little Colvin?"

"I don't know. Yeah, I guess so."

"I don't like it," Jake said.

"What's wrong with it?"

"I don't know. Can't see clear to put my finger on it exactly. Something about you though, not her. Whatever's eating her'll be all right when she gets married and has a couple of kids. What's eating you ain't gonna be so easy to get rid of."

"Me?" Carter said. "Me? There's nothing the hell wrong with me!"

Jake sighed. "That's a good sign of it too. Jumping down my throat the minute I suggest it. It's you, all right."

"You better get some rest," Carter said.

"I guess you don't like the life you're living," Jake said. "I always had a feeling you weren't night people. It don't fit you somehow. You need an alarm in the mornings and putting the cat out at night. I've seen it in you since you were a kid. I reckon that's what worries me about Colvin.

124

I can't figure whether it's her you want or daylight. Can you?"

"You better try to sleep."

"Hush up. I'll sleep in a minute. I got to try to say something to you first. Sober for the first time in about twenty years I reckon, so I better say it. Folks ain't ever what they seem like. That's the thing. They've all got a little picture of themselves like they'd like to be and they live like that picture. You know what I mean. Will, he's the tough boy, your mammy, she's the great mother of the world. Me, the philosopher of Maynard County café life. That's why I like your little Colvin. She ain't got set in a picture of herself yet. Maybe she never will. It's the folks that don't live the best. The thing is, that little picture is what you get to accept about people. And it's nothing but a mask. It's just like a Halloween false face or one of those damned black things they put on at Mardi Gras. What's on the other side don't often show through and when it does it ain't ever very pretty. You remember ole Ferguson and that time with the nigger? That's what I mean about what's on the other side."

"What's all this got to do with me and Laura?" Carter said. He lit another cigarette.

"Well, what's on the other side of your mask?" Jake said.

"I don't even know what the mask is," Carter said.

Jake laughed again. "No, I guess you don't," he said. "You don't really see that picture of noble restraint you trot out for folks, do you?"

"O.K.," Carter said. "Put the knife up. Where you leading up to?"

Jake was silent, his eyes closed, for a long moment. When he spoke again his voice was hesitant, unsure, wavered by the effect of drugs and time. "There was something special worrying me," he said. "Can't seem to get hold of it."

"Go to sleep, Uncle Jake," Carter said. "Time enough in the morning."

Jake's eyes opened. "No. Want to get it said. Sober for the first time. I know." His head moved, he tried to raise up from the pillow, but Carter pushed him back down.

"Lie still, Uncle Jake," he said.

"I know," Jake said again. "It's Julie Hobson. That business. That's gonna get to Laura Lee. You ought to do something about that."

Carter shook his head. "You're not making sense, Uncle Jake," he said. "Go on to sleep."

"Yes," Jake said. "Yes, I am. It's Sonny Colvin. You remember him, Carter?"

"Vaguely."

"You know what he does, don't you?"

"I know he's up north somewhere."

"That's right. On the east coast. With Sherman Green."

"The hell you say." Carter got up from the chair and stood looking down at Jake in astonishment.

"I thought you didn't know it," Jake said with satisfaction. "I knew that little gal of yours didn't. I reckon she figures Sonny's about the only one of her folks that ever amounted to anything. I guess he's important to her for that reason whether she likes him or not. That's the thing, Carter. You know it ain't been easy on her, living with Irene. You know what Irene is. And that old man, dreaming his life away in a rocking chair. You don't want her knowing about Sonny too sudden. You ought to see she finds it out in some way so it don't make no difference to her."

"But what's it got to do with Julie?" Carter said.

"That's who she is," Jake said. "She's Colvin's girl. He sent her down here to sit on something for him. I don't know what. Evidence of some kind against somebody, I guess. Either that or he's got her out of town to keep her from being subpoenaed by a committee. But that's what she's doing here. Jackson Ferguson ain't as big a fool as Sonny thinks. He's lived up north so long he's ready to sneer at everybody down here and it ain't all that easy. Something's gonna happen. You ought to see about it. Been trying to tell you this, but I keep forgetting. I forget a lot lately." He mumbled incoherently for a moment and Carter leaned over the bed trying to understand him. Then he spoke clearly again, the words loud in the little room. "Will," he said. "You ought to watch that Will."

Carter stared down at him. He heard the words, but he couldn't make sense of them. He thought, Arlie and Julie. Surely not. He thought, Laura. He looked down at Jake. "You sure about this?" he said. But Jake was asleep, his hands crossed peacefully on the clean white sheet.

126

Carter stood still, staring down at his uncle, feeling the thoughts dashing and smashing against his head, fragmented, forming quick pictures that vanished in collision with word images. Laura. She and her brother in a T-model, driving out of town to swim in a lake of moonlight. Julie, fugitive. Julie smiling at Arlie. Jackson Ferguson, walking his streets in darkness. Will, yelling as Arlie pushed him out the door. All of them wearing black and yellow slashed masks, posturing in midnight on an empty stage. He shook his head.

Outside the door, Will pushed away from the wall and walked down the hall. He was smiling.

Irene Colvin threw the empty bottle into the street, hearing the shattering glass on the curbstone with a feeling of satisfaction. She lit a cigarette. Around her the neighborhood was dark. There was a light on the corner and, farther away, the light at the railway crossing. That was all. She stood up and went to the porch railing, peering into the dark. She wondered how long Laura was going to stay out. Not that it mattered. She was sure she wasn't sleeping with Carter McCain. She didn't think Laura had enough to her to sleep with him or with anybody else.

Irene Colvin didn't really like her daughter. She thought she loved her, because she was hers and had once been a beautiful baby with long blonde curls and a way of turning her head to one side, but she didn't like her. She didn't like her because she didn't understand her and Irene Colvin had no use for the people she didn't understand. She lumped them together as goody-goodies or bourgeois, or fools. The people she thought she understood were all the lost, but she didn't know that. She believed in the unalterable fact that she lived a doomed life on a doomed planet and she had no use for the people who by scratching and sweating and fighting denied it. She didn't think it should be denied.

Her picture of Irene Colvin was that of the rebel. She saw herself spending the little they forgot and gave us in a moment of weakness. And behind her mask was the uncontrollable rage of a lifetime in which nothing she'd wanted had ever worked out right, not once. There are no rebels without a cause. The cause is hate.

She walked across the porch to the swing and pushed it back and forth sullenly. "All asleep," she said aloud. "Pigs. Pigs. Sleeping it all away." She went into the house and began to go through the cabinets and drawers methodically. She was sure she'd put a half pint away somewhere the last time she'd been sobering up. She put the coffeepot on to heat while she searched for it, not hearing the coffee begin to boil, then spatter onto the stove, then erupt violently against the top of the pot until it all boiled away. Only when the scorched smell began to permeate the house did she remember it and go back to the kitchen to take the ruined pot from the stove. She threw it into the garbage can, splattering the wall with grounds, listening to the sizzle against the porcelain, looking down in astonishment at the burn across her right hand. "Damn them," she said sullenly. "Damn them. Damn them. Damn them."

"I'm going to leave in the morning," Julie said. She stood against the sink in Arlie's kitchen, watching him as he sat across a kitchen chair, resting his arms on the back.

"I know it," he said. He looked straight at her. "I've known it all night. What is it? That fellow that got off the train?"

"Yes, in one way. No, in the way you mean."

"So," he said. "It's been real."

"I love you," Julie said. "Please take it and know it. I love you. I haven't ever loved anybody else. Not once in all my life since my father died."

"Sure," Arlie said.

"No. Please. Listen to me, Arlie. It's more important than anything else in the world has ever been to me. Maybe it is the most important thing in the world, period. I don't know. But please listen."

"I'm listening." He had not moved, nor taken his eyes from her face.

"We have to believe in something, haven't we?" Julie said.

"Not necessarily."

"Yes we have. Something. Even if it's nothing. So here's what I believe. I believe in you and me. It's not much to go a lifetime toward and after, these few months, but it's enough for me. It's got to be. So don't take it away from me. Don't spoil it all and poison it all. And kill it. You hear me?"

"All right."

"You're not listening. Please listen. I love you. What I mean by that, I don't know. More than wanting to go to bed with you, more than feeling happy when I'm with you, more than wishing I could stay forever. More than that. I mean I'd love you no matter what happened, no matter what you did, no matter how it ended. Yes, even if you do poison it and kill it I'll love you—so much that jealousy and hate and fear and pride and death can't touch it. You hear me?"

"I hear you."

"And I tell you it's the only hope. The only hope for me or you or anybody else. It's what's going to save the world. Do you remember what I told you about Orwell's *1984?* How they force the lovers to deny each other by threatening them with the thing they fear the most? Orwell used that to show the destruction of everything good in the world, but it isn't true. It won't do it. Because love can take denial. The way I love you I can betray you and deny you and it won't stop. You can betray me and it won't stop. Because nobody can expect another human being to be more than human. It isn't fair to expect it. And if we love enough we don't. So we can take the betrayal and the denial. And the love goes on. You hear me?"

"How are you going to betray me, Julie?"

She began to cry then, quietly, the tears running down her face without her noticing them. "I'm leaving. I told you."

"Is that all?"

"That's all. That's enough."

"Yes," he said. "I guess it is." He got up. "Let's take Laura and Estelle back down to Dupree's," he said.

"All right." She went in front of him to the living room. Estelle lay on the sofa asleep, her legs curled under her. Laura sat by the window, looking down onto the empty square. "We're going," Julie said. She shook Estelle. "Get up, Essie," she said. "I'm going to take you back where you belong."

Estelle sat up. "You were going to stay with me," she said sleepily, her eyes wide and alarmed.

"I'm taking you back to Dupree," Julie said. "It's where

129

you belong." She looked at Laura. "Come on, Laura," she said. "We'll find Carter."

She didn't look at Arlie again. She opened the door and went down the stairs to the street.

4.

JACKSON FERGUSON watched Will McCain get out of the pickup truck and walk toward him. He didn't move to come forward to greet him. He stood still against the corner lamppost and let him come.

Will stopped ten yards away. "Mr. Ferguson?" he said, his voice loud on the air of coming morning.

"Yes," Ferguson said. He put one hand on his blackjack, then, feeling its reassuring weight, thought, It's about ole Jake McCain. "How is Jake, boy?" he said.

"Resting," Will said. "Resting. There's something I got to talk to you about."

"All right," Ferguson said. He moved forward so that he could see the boy's face. He looked intent and solemn in the half-light of the street lamps, but his eyes were laughing.

He's having me on, too, Jackson thought.

"I got some information I reckon you could use," Will said.

"All right," Ferguson said. "It's your duty to report to The Law. What is it?" He waited.

Will took another step forward. "It's about that Julie Hobson," he said.

Goddamn, Jackson thought. Goddamn it all. I have sat here for six months trying to place that girl and now in one night they are telling me from all directions what a fool I've been. "I know all there needs to be known about Julie Hobson," he said.

Will's eyes narrowed and Jackson watched him, thinking, That one could turn mean. He could turn mean quick. I'll have to file him.

"It seems to me," Will said. "The Law ought to take an interest in things citizens can tell 'em. I reckon I could go to Thurston with it, but I figured you was the man in charge. I figured you'd do something about it."

"I aim to," Jackson said.

"You mean you know?" Will said. "You mean to tell me you've known all the time who that girl is and ain't done nothing about it? Why, Mr. Ferguson, that don't seem quite right to me. You reckon what them guys up north would think about a thing like that if they knew it. I figure she's up to something pretty big sitting around here for a whole spring and summer. I figure she or something she's carrying must be pretty hot. Seems to me like a big man like you would want to pick her up and hold her. Seems like you'd at least want to talk to them Feds about it."

Ferguson moved forward. "Are you going to shut up, boy?" he said quietly. "Don't you know we lawmen have got ways and means of doing things? Don't you reckon if you start blabbing your mouth off before I'm ready for you to I could have you up for obstructing justice? Don't you reckon that?" He was raging inside but he kept his voice calm and level. "From where I stand," he went on, "I figure that you ought to just keep your mouth shut." He moved closer.

"Sure, sure, Mr. Ferguson." Will took a step backwards. "I ain't criticizing your methods or nothing. I just thought I knew something you'd like to hear about. That's all." He moved another step toward his truck.

Yellow, Jackson thought. Yellow too. As well as being a smart aleck. He walked over to the truck and stood close to the door while Will got in. "I figure I know how to run my business," he said again. "You just keep quiet like I tell you and don't go spoiling the way I got things set up. You hear me?"

"I hear you," Will said. He started the motor and backed out, leaving Ferguson in the middle of the street staring after him.

He would have to do something now, Ferguson thought, wondering in the instant of thinking it if there had ever been a doubt that he would do something. He knew there had. It would have been easy. Forget he'd seen Bagley get off the train and they'd be gone by another night. Because that was what Bagley was doing here. He'd come for her. Whatever the purpose of her sojourn, it was over, at least as far as Bellefonte was concerned. She wouldn't be here another night. He had only to ignore that shadow on the train platform for a few more hours—maybe only till daylight—and that would be the end of it. But he couldn't now. Will McCain knew and if he knew there were others who knew and there was Thurston Marlow and the new bunch in City Hall. There wasn't anything he could do about it. He'd have to arrest her. It would be easy, hold her on an open charge, suspicion of conspirarcy, anything. He knew who she was. He knew she was a cohort of known criminals. That would be enough for Thurston, for Thurston who was only waiting for the chance, the slip, the reason to smile and say, "Ferguson's getting old." He remembered Thurston's face on the night of the Halloween fiasco, smiling, waiting. The waiting could stop now. He would have his opening. He might even go so far as to intimate some connection between Sonny Colvin and Ferguson and that girl, some collusion between them because of that damned nigger. And if he started looking into that God knew what he'd come up with.

He started on around the block, looking up toward Arlie's apartment. The lights were out there now. He stopped still, staring up at the blank windows. Then he went on down the block. I can at least make one more circuit, he thought. I've got time for that.

"Dupree," Julie said. "You ought to close on up and take Essie here home." She was sitting on a stool at the counter. Estelle and Laura sat one on each side of her like figures in a ceremonial frieze.

"You said you'd stay," Estelle said. She looked small and frightened and vulnerable, Julie thought. But all the more reason then.

"You ought to be with Dupree," Julie said.

Dupree leaned across the counter and put his hand on Estelle's cheek. "I'm here, baby," he said.

Estelle began to cry and Dupree came around the counter and put his arms around her. "It's going to be all right," he said. "It's going to be all right."

He had hated the thought of what Estelle was doing.

He'd rejected it from his mind, sending Carter with her, paying for it because beyond the hate and repugnance he loved Estelle and he didn't want to lose her. But he had put a wall between them with the gesture. He'd denied her with the giving of the money. Now it didn't matter. It was over. Finished. To be forgotten. He'd take care of her through this morning and this day and this week. And afterwards it would be different. There are ways of loving that are more important than holding on to something. Maybe Essie would learn that too. He looked at Julie over Estelle's shoulder. "I thank you," he said. "For watching out for her. And for bringing her home."

"She's a good kid," Julie said. "Aren't you, Es? You go on home with Dupree, why don't you? It's getting real late now. It'll soon be morning. It'll soon be daylight." She slid off the stool and went to look out onto the empty street in front of the café. "I can feel the sun ready to come up out there now," she said. "It's just a few seconds away, waiting. Look at the street, waiting. It's the time of night when the nervous people can at last give in and go on to sleep. Nothing of the night is going to happen to them now. They'll sleep in sunlight like the tree people used to do."

She walked back to Dupree and Estelle and handed Dupree the bottle of codeine. "This is for Essie," she said. "They say two every four hours, but it's safe to cheat a little."

"Julie," Arlie said. He was standing against the jukebox, watching her. "Come on, Julie."

"All right," she said. "Laura Lee, we'll take you out to the hospital. We'll take you to Carter."

Laura slid off the stool. "Maybe I ought to go on home," she said.

Julie shook her head. "I don't intend to abandon my charges." She laughed, the sound strained and high. "I feel like Noah," she said. "He called them two by two."

"Hush, Julie," Arlie said.

"All right." She walked over to him and put her hand on his shoulder. "Let's take Laura Lee out to Carter."

The door opened and shut, the sound turning them all toward it. Will stood just inside the door, smiling at them. "Good morning, people," he said. He walked over to Dupree and Estelle, who were still standing with their arms

134

around each other. "What's the matter with you two?" he said.

"Give him some coffee, Annie," Dupree said to the waitress. She was sitting behind the coffee urn half asleep, her chin propped on her fist. She got up slowly. "Want coffee, Will?" she said.

"Sure." He sat down at the counter. Laura Lee moved back a little away from him.

They all watched him warily as though they were waiting for him to say something although none of them could have said what it was they expected or wanted or dreaded for him to say.

Julie broke the silence. "Well, I forgot that one," she said. "I really should have planned something for him."

Will swung around on the stool. He faced her, propping his elbows on the counter behind him, still smiling. "Julie," he said. "Julie Hobson. Don't worry about me, baby. I've found what I was looking for. Don't worry about Will McCain. I would say, going on the evidence, that it's Julie Hobson we'd better all get together and worry about."

Behind her Julie could feel Arlie stiffen. She put her hand on his arm. "Cut it out, Will," he said quietly.

Will shook his head. "Uh-huh," he said. "I been waiting for this a long time now and I figure to say it." He turned around and picked up his coffee cup, turning back to face them, holding the cup in his right hand. "Blackjack is around yonder on the south side of the square about now," he said. "He walks pretty slow, but he walks steady. When he gets right about here he's going to come in here after his hourly cup of joe. If I was you, Julie, I'd be gone when he gets here."

"What kind of crap are you talking, Will?" Dupree said.

Arlie put Julie behind him and stepped forward. "O.K., Will," he said. "Say all of it. Come on. Say it all and be sure you're finished because I'm going to fix it so you won't say anything else for some time to come."

Will laughed. "I told you," he said. "I said it. You better get Julie out of here. Because Blackjack's on the way, and Blackjack knows who she is." He watched Arlie's face. Then he laughed again. "By God," he said. "I don't think you know. This is going to be a hell of a lot better than I thought."

"Get out of here, Will," Dupree said. "Get on out. I ain't
135

in any mood for you to start any trouble. I'm gonna close up in a few minutes anyway. Go home."

"O.K., Will," Julie said quietly. "Tell him."

Will looked at her, measuring her calm face. "Don't nothing ever faze you?" he said. "Nothing? Ever?" He looked away from her angrily. "I'll tell you who she is, Arlie," he said. "She's a gun moll. Your precious little piece is nothing but a part of the east coast combine. Nothing else. She's Sonny Colvin's girl. Not Arlie Machen's; Sonny Colvin's. And don't start beating me up yet because there's gonna be proof of it through that door yonder at any minute."

Arlie stood still. Slowly his hands unclenched and fell at his sides. He didn't have to turn and look at Julie. He didn't have to do anything. He stood still.

"Arlie," Julie said behind him. "I'll go now."

He turned slowly toward her, looking carefully into her face. Then he nodded. "I'll go with you," he said.

"You don't have to."

"You forgetting all those things you said up at the place?" he said. "I have to."

She smiled, her eyes lighting for a moment. "Thank you," she said. "But I'm not going anywhere."

Estelle had stepped away from Dupree. Her eyes were shining. "Golly, Julie," she said softly. "Goll-ee."

Dupree shook his head at her. "Baby," he said sadly. "Nothing but a damned baby." He put his hand on her hair. "What can we do to help you, Julie?" he said.

Julie shook her head. "This is mine," she said. "Go on home with Es."

"I could get him in here and keep him busy awhile," Dupree said. "You can go out the back door and I'll get Annie to drive my car around there. You can be halfway to Hunter City before he knows it."

"He can call Hunter City," Julie said. "He can call Chattanooga, or Newcastle, or Atlanta. And there's Bagley, a sitting duck over in that hotel. There's nothing I can do. Except maybe get rid of a few things . . ."

"Bagley?" Dupree said. "Bagley?"

Julie shrugged. "He came for me," she said.

Laura Lee made a strangled sound. She had been standing pressed back against the counter, listening. When Will had first made his statement it hadn't made any sense to

136

her. She couldn't put together the disparate parts of Julie and her brother and the east coast combine, a name in TV detective series. It made no sense. She couldn't understand the sudden intrusion of her brother's name here in this restaurant of night people, here with the dawn waiting outside to take her back to another world, here alone in darkness. Sonny? she thought desperately. Sonny? And Julie? What does he mean? She watched them, seeing the concern and fear on their faces, and she knew it did mean something—something bad—to all of them. She shook her head. When they began talking about getting Julie away she knew it was serious and true and that somehow she had been living among all of them without knowing anything about them. It was like tuning in one of those TV programs in the middle of the hour. There were a bunch of people on the stage but she couldn't figure out how they'd gotten there or who they were or what their relationship was with each other. She tried to say something and the words stuck so that only the sound came, a lost sort of sound that made her listen to herself as though she too were somebody strange.

They all looked at her.

"Oh, God," Julie said. "Laura. Laura Lee. Honey."

Arlie grabbed her arm. "You ain't got time to fix it with her," he said. "I'll do it. I'll do it tomorrow. Now I want you to do what I tell you."

Julie shook him off. "It's important," she said. "It's awfully important. Laura."

Laura Lee shook her head, staring at Julie. "Is it true what he said? Is Sonny a crook? Are you Sonny's girl?"

"In a way, honey," Julie said. "But only in a way. You see . . ."

Laura didn't hear her. She began to run. Julie could see the running start in her before she'd made a movement. She was already running inside her head, running from all of them, from the truth, from herself. Julie reached behind her and opened the door.

"What are you doing?" Arlie said.

"Do you want her to run right through it?" Julie said dully. She stood to one side and watched Laura Lee run into the darkness before daylight, the white dress vanishing into the shadows down the street. She felt very tired suddenly, and old. She wanted to go after Laura, to stop her, to keep the running out of her by a sheer effort of will, to save her as she hadn't been able to save herself. But she couldn't. Either Laura would save herself or she wouldn't. It was that simple. Old John Caple had come after her on a nighttime beach in Virginia once, but he hadn't stopped her. You can only stop running by an effort of will of your own. She focused her eyes on Arlie.

"Where is she going?" Arlie said.

Julie shook her head. "Nowhere," she said. "Where does everybody run to? You see her tomorrow. You hear me? You talk to her. You've got to get Carter to talk to her." She said the useless words carefully, knowing the futility involved in them, knowing too the necessity of saying them.

"Yes," Arlie said. "But listen to me. Listen now. Listen good. I say it once. Go on out back and get whatever you got to get and get Bagley and take my car and get the hell out of town."

"I told you, it won't work."

Arlie looked at her. "It will work," he said. "He will not send out a report on my car. I promise you. Go on."

"Arlie?" Julie said. "Come with me?"

He shook his head. "I have to stay to stop him," he said. "I can stop him. Believe that. I can."

"Arlie," Julie said "Don't . . . don't do anything . . ."

"No. Not anything like that. I promise you. Tomorrow night will come like always with Jackson Ferguson walking the block. Go on now. Do like I tell you. It won't work with you around. You got to go."

"What is it?"

"It don't matter what, Julie. I just happen to have something I can use for you now. I got something to give you. I want to give it. Because in spite of everything—maybe because of it—I believe in what you were telling me up yonder tonight. I guess I won't ever see you again, Julie. But in a funny sort of way it doesn't matter. You go on now."

"Arlie." She was crying now, the tears falling unheeded. Arlie reached up and brushed them away with his fingers. "So long, Julie," he said. He turned and walked out the front door of the café into the streets of night.

"Come on," Dupree said. "This way." He went to the back of the café and Julie followed him. She ducked under the curtain in the archway and picked her way through the piles of cartons and discarded chairs and went on out the back door.

"What the hell do all you folks think you're doing?" Will said when Dupree came back. "You trying to obstruct justice?"

Dupree stared at him. "I thought I told you to get the hell out of my place of business," he said. "If you don't I reckon I can find something to keep ole Ferguson busy with myself."

"O.K., O.K.," Will said. "Don't get in an uproar. I'm going. I'm going." He finished his coffee and put the cup on the counter. "What I can't figure out," he said, standing up and tucking his shirt into his pants, "is what the hell it is that makes all you folks stick together?"

Dupree laughed. "No, Will," he said. "I reckon you can't." He turned his back on Will and began going through the night's receipts stacked in a neat pile beside the cash register. "Sit down, Essie," he said. "We'll go home in a minute."

"All right, Dupree," Estelle said. She came around the counter and drew herself a cup of coffee, looking thoughtful. "Don't you reckon somebody ought to go after Laura?" she said.

Dupree looked at her. "That's a good idea, baby," he said. "I sort of figured Carter to be in any minute. We'll do something then. But it's right good of you to think about it. Drink your coffee." He continued to check the receipts against the cash, working slowly and methodically at the job he'd chosen to live by.

Julie picked her way through the debris of the alley behind the café and walked out on the street across from the filling station. Looking toward the square she could see nothing but darkness, though it had lightened now in preparation for the false dawn. She went across the street without looking again and got into Arlie's car. The tank was full, he kept it that way. She reached under the glove compartment and untaped the extra key she knew he kept there. She worried about starting the motor in the stillness, but it was something she couldn't do anything about, so she turned the key and drove toward the highway.

She made the trip to her room fast. The ledgers were

still locked in the briefcase—all the neat meticulous accounts in Sonny's neat meticulous hand, the figures and letters for the tax lawyer, the neat beautiful shifts and balances that made a dry-cleaning business cover neatly the monies made in the little room behind the coats and cloaks on wire hangers. The records, Sonny's records and Julie Hobson's passport. Her passport for running, her reason for being, her ticket to somewhere else.

At the hotel she left the motor running and ran through the empty lobby to the desk, looking quickly underneath the counter and flipping the book to the only entry for the day: K. D. Bagley, Providence. Room 202. She went up the stairs and banged with the flat of her hand on the door.

Bagley came out of sleep in one instant, grabbing the suit from its hanger and getting into it as he came to the door. "Julie?" he said.

"Get the lead out," she said. "We're rolling."

He opened the door and followed her down the stairs. "My suit didn't get dry," he said petulantly, scratching at his back.

"Damn your suit," Julie said. "Sonny made a major miscalculation on that hick deputy."

They got into the car. "How you know he ain't got a bulletin out on this buggy?" Bagley said as they turned onto the highway and headed west. "Where'd you get it?"

"It's all right," Julie said. "No thanks to you or Sonny. Now shut up and let me drive. I intend to put a state between me and Bellefonte before noon."

"You got them papers?" Bagley said, settling back against the seat.

"Stupid," Julie said sharply. "I got the papers first. If I'd had to leave anything it would have been you."

"O.K., O.K.," Bagley said. "Wake me up in New Orleans." He shut his eyes.

There was nothing stirring yet along the highway although the false dawn gave the sky a half-light, pushing up against the black ceiling with promise. They passed the filling stations and drive-ins and the lumber company, its smokestack throwing a faint blue mist into the early air. Then there were the outlying houses and the fences and the roadside posters, and finally the long hill with the

VFW crosses marking the traffic deaths, and Bellefonte was gone.

Julie settled back in the seat and began to drive seriously. Ten miles out they met a loaded truck, taking a hill slowly and steadily in the predawn emptiness of highway. Her foot touched the dimmer and she slowed the car. When the truck passed her she raised one hand toward it and tapped the horn lightly in highway greeting. The driver answered her, the sound loud and clear and lonely in the lightening dark. Then the truck was gone behind her. She kept her eyes on the road and drove steadily and carefully and right on the speed limit. She passed the first road sign. Hunter City. Twenty-five miles.

Arlie stepped out onto the street. The square was empty. The moon was down. Overhead the stars, paling with the false dawn, winked dimly. There was a breeze, stirring lightly the maples on the courthouse lawn. Their rustle was the only sound. He listened, thinking in the stillness that he would be able to hear the footsteps from the other side of the square. But of course he could not. Those footsteps must be coming slowly. He visualized their maker, tall in the darkness, stopping to look in doorways and alleyways, trying the doors of buildings for the hundredth time, checking his watch against the clock in the locker-plant window. Unhurried, sure, with no need of hurry. Because his quarry was waiting, unwarned, unarmed. A girl, alone in the night.

But you forgot about love, Mr. Ferguson. And loyalty and faith and all the things you've spent a lifetime denying, he thought. You just plain didn't think about that. Now you'll have to. Now after thirty years you will have to think about that. He smiled to himself. He had thought this was going to cost him something. He had thought he was making, for Julie and for himself, the last and greatest sacrifice. Now, looking across the empty square of stone and brick, looking into the trees stirring with the late-early wind, he felt almost triumphant. He felt that he was laying down, at last, something that had hampered him. He thought of Julie's karma as he walked toward the courthouse lawn, stepping slowly and quietly with Indian grace.

At the bandstand he stopped, looking across the lawn

toward the other side of the square, waiting. After a minute he made out the shape in the darkness.

Jackson Ferguson, if he was moving at all, was moving so slowly that he seemed to stand still. Arlie watched him, puzzled. He was in front of the hardware store now. Arlie moved out toward the street light on the corner of the lawn and he could see him plainly. He wasn't moving. He was standing still on the corner, his hands at his sides, looking down the east side of the square. Toward . . . what? Arlie couldn't tell. Only that it was in the direction of his garage and the post office and the paper, in the direction of the corner traffic lights. He could be watching anything.

As he watched, Ferguson began to move. He walked up to the intersection and looked both ways up and down the empty streets before starting across under the dead traffic light.

Arlie waited until he was in the middle of the intersection, lighted by the corner lampposts, alone in the middle of a four-way intersection, caught in electric light. Then he moved forward to the edge of the lawn and raised his voice on the dead air of four o'clock.

"Father?" he called into the emptiness. "Father?"

The shadow stopped, hesitated, then started forward off the intersection. Arlie stepped under the street lamp and called again. "Father," he called clearly and loudly into the morning. "Father. I've got something I want to say to you."

5.

WILL sat in his truck in front of the café. He was waiting for Carter. He saw Arlie come out and go across the square, but he wasn't interested in where he was going now. He was through with Arlie. He could see Dupree getting ready to close the café and Estelle, sitting on a stool drinking coffee, waiting for him. He didn't care about that either. He was waiting for Carter now, waiting to drop the last piece of his homemade bomb on his last enemy and so be quits of the whole damned bunch of them. Forever. He leaned back against the seat and waited.

Carter left the hospital and drove back to town slowly, trying to think about what he had to do. He thought of Laura Lee and was surprised to find that he felt irritated with her. There was, he felt, no reason for her to have to be protected. It wasn't fair that he should have to do it. She was a grown woman. She should be able to hear a simple fact about her brother without it doing anything to the essential being she was. He knew this way of thinking was unfair, but he couldn't help it. He was mad at her for her coldness at Arlie's, when he'd had to go go to the hospital, and he was madder now because he'd have to be patient and understanding and try to tell her a damned simple fact that would probably upset hell out of her. He thought of the things his uncle had said to him—a mask hiding the real things underneath. So maybe it was true. Maybe he wasn't understanding or gentle or helpful or any damned other thing. Because suddenly now, driving toward Laura and the responsibility she was beginning to become for him, he didn't want to be understanding, or helpful, or gentle. He wanted to shake her. He wanted to say, Who gives a damn if your brother is Public Enemy No. 1 or your mother the whore of the world? You're you, Laura Lee. And what you make of yourself is yours, nobody else's, and to hell with it all.

He drove through the square and into the parking space in front of the café. Looking down the street he saw that Arlie's windows were dark and he got out of the car, expecting to see them inside the café. But he never got inside. Will climbed out of the truck and stopped him. "You looking for somebody?" he said.

"Not you," Carter said, starting to walk around him.

"Wait a minute," Will said. He moved in front of him. "I got something to tell you."

"I haven't got time," Carter said. "I got to find Laura Lee."

"That's what I got to tell you something about," Will said.

Carter turned toward him. "What are you talking about?" he said. "What the hell are you starting now? Where is she? Isn't she in there?" He nodded toward the restaurant.

Will shook his head slowly from side to side. "Nope," he said. "She's not there." He smiled. "None of 'em's there, except Dupree and Es—if you want to count them. They've all dispersed, Carter. All dispersed."

"Come on, Will," Carter said. "It's late and I'm tired. Cut the crap and tell me what the hell you're talking about."

"That's all I been getting tonight," Will said. "All you folks sure seem anxious to hear bad news."

"Where's Laura?" Carter said.

"Well," Will said. "You might say nobody knows. You might just say she flew the coop."

"What happened?" Carter said, dread coming up to match the irritation in him.

"I don't know," Will said. "Nothing much. Everybody around here seems to take things so hard. I just come in there and they was all sitting around drinking that swill of Dupree's. I come in with a straightforward, honest-to-God warning for Miss Julie that ole Blackjack had heard

144

about her and was coming after her, and damned if they all didn't start acting like a bunch of chickens with their heads cut off. You know it's real funny." He laughed shortly. "I plum got the idea none of them had known beforehand nothing about ole Julie or that Sonny Colvin or anything else."

Carter stared at him. "Then where the hell," he said slowly, "did you find out about it?"

"Well," Will said. "You might say the hearing's pretty good in these hospital corridors. Nothing to stop the sound . . ."

"Damn you," Carter said. "Damn you to hell, Will. Brother or not. Where did Laura Lee go?"

"That's what I'm trying to tell you," Will said. "If you'd just calm down a minute. Nobody knows where she went. She went tearing off out the door like somebody crazy. Just running. Not going nowhere particular it looked like, just running. That Julie she wanted to do something about it, I think, but she had to beat it out of here in something of a hurry. And Arlie, he's over there on the square doing some sort of blackmail job on The Blackjack, near as I can figure."

"Which direction did she run in?" Carter said.

Will jerked his head. "Down that way," he said.

"Toward home," Carter said. "Maybe she just went home. There's that possibility."

"Yeah," Will said. "She's got such a hell of a lot to go home to. I can't think of nothing better than for her to go home and tell Mama all about Sonny boy. Can you?"

Carter stopped his fist in the instant of drawing back on Will, and turned toward his cab. "There ain't no time now for you and me, Will," he said. "But we've had it. You just remember that." He slammed the door and backed into the road.

I got to find her, he thought. If I don't find her, God knows what the hell might happen to her. But why me, damn it? Why me? How the hell did I ever get mixed up in a thing like this?

Will stood for a moment, looking after Carter. Then he shrugged, got back in the truck, and went home.

The house was dark except for a light over the carport, but after he'd put the truck away and gone into the house he saw that there was a light on in the kitchen and he walked back toward it.

His mother was sitting at the kitchen table drinking a cup of coffee. "Willie?" she said when she heard him in the living room. "That you?"

"Yessum." He came on into the kitchen.

The light on the kitchen range was on, throwing a small spot of light over the stove. The rest of the room was in darkness. "Where you been so late?" Bertha said.

"We run into a little trouble," Will said.

"What kind of trouble?"

It's Uncle Jake," Will said. "Me and Carter had to take him to the hospital."

"Oh, Lord," Bertha said. She stood up, pulling her robe around her. "I'll get dressed and you can just take me out there. It's the old fool's heart, of course. I knew it. I've been telling him for twenty years if he didn't quit swilling corn like a damned pig he'd end up just like this. Don't you go off to bed now. I want you to take me in."

Will propped his foot on a kitchen chair. "The doctor said for us to let him get some sleep and rest through the night," he said mildly.

"You mean there ain't nobody out there with him?" Bertha said. She looked at Will closely. "Where's Carter?"

"Why should I know where Carter is?" Will said. "I ain't taken him to raise. I don't know nothing about Carter."

Bertha went to the wall switch and flipped on the overhead light. The harsh glare fell across them, shining into Will's eyes so that he blinked and put one hand up to shield them. Bertha put out her hand, moved Will's away from his face. "What you done to Carter?" she said.

"What's the matter with you, Mama?" Will said. "Why you ask me something like that? What on earth would make you think I've done anything to Carter? Hell. Carter lives his life and I live mine. I don't know nothing about him."

Bertha continued to look at him. "Don't lie to me, Will," she said. "You ain't ever been able to lie to me. I see right into you. What have you done to Carter?"

"Jesus, Mama. Stop it. Carter's been out to the hospital with me and Uncle Jake. Now he's gone somewhere after Laura Lee. I don't know where. Over at her house, I reckon. I don't know. Turn that light off, please. It's hurting my eyes."

"How come he had to go anywhere after Laura Lee?" Bertha said relentlessly. "I thought Laura Lee was with him. What you done to that girl?"

"Nothing. Nothing," Will said angrily. "Leave me alone."

Bertha sat down in the chair and looked at Will, shaking her head. "You might as well go on and tell me," she said. "Your daddy'll be in in another hour and he'll get it out of you. So you might better just go on and tell me."

Will looked at her. "It was nothing," he said. "Nothing. I heard Blackjack was after Julie Hobson 'cause she was that Sonny Colvin's girl and up to some hanky-panky for him here and I warned her to get out of here. That is all. Period."

"You trying to tell me that Colvin boy's some sort of crook?" Bertha said.

"That's right," Will said. He felt more confident suddenly and he smiled a little, relaxing. "Mr. High-and-mighty Colvin nothing but a handyman for Sherman Green and that Julie nothing but a handywoman for him."

"Hush," Bertha said. "Hush up. You mean you told Laura Lee that? And Carter wasn't even there with her? That's what you mean, isn't it?"

"Well, yeah. I guess so. But Carter's gone after her. She run off somewhere but Carter's gone hunting her. Funny thing. He acted sort of put out with her too, same as with me. Isn't that funny?"

"Oh, Lord," Bertha said again. She got up and walked up and down the kitchen for a minute, frowning, trying to piece together what she knew about her son and about Laura Lee and about all the people of all her life. There had been a lot of them, the desperate and anxious, the happy and afraid, who came to her door in the hours of night to purchase the hope in the bottle. She'd learned a lot about them in those years, a lot that had helped her often in dealing with people, a lot she wished in this moment she didn't know.

She stopped and looked at Will. He sat still under the overhead bulb, looking at her. In his face she saw only satisfaction and relief and something that might be greed. She sighed. He was her son. She had done the best she could with both him and Carter, but it was about over. What she could do and couldn't do had passed—the mistakes she'd made, the right things she might have done. All had jelled, set, become the two men who still lived under this roof but were her children no more.

There was one last thing. So she did that. "You still want in those paratroopers, Will?" she said.

She watched his face light up, the smile and the greed wiping everything else away. "I sure the hell do," he said.

"I'll sign the papers tomorrow," she said. "Don't worry about your daddy. He'll do what I say."

Now dawn was coming. The blackness that fell after the false dawn was lifting, becoming a grayness in the east, soon to be rose and gold and blue; then the day. The wind was up, blowing a little now, cooling a little now, before the heat of day.

In a cottage on the lake Dr. Charles Kent sat impatiently on the screened front porch, watching the road. There was no sign of the small car belonging to Betty Dawson, no lights came through the woodland where the road left the highway. Nothing stirred except the trees in the morning wind. He lit a cigarette and looked at his watch. In a few moments now he would have to go on back home. It would be day. Time for his wife and children to get up and turn on the Today show and stuff themselves on cornflakes. He got up and went down to the shoreline, standing for a few moments, watching the lake begin to turn gray in front of him. Then he turned and went back to his car and drove home.

Betty Dawson had been relieved by the morning nurse an hour before. She was at home in bed, sleeping the soundest sleep she'd slept in five years. Beside her on the night table was an envelope addressed to the University Medical School in Newcastle asking for a position in the city system. She slept in a pink gown with a high-necked collar and her face was scrubbed very clean and shiny with soap and water.

Dupree and Estelle sat together in the living room of their house. They had washed the dishes together and dusted the living room. Estelle said she figured she ought to be doing something. Now they sat silent on the brocaded sofa, holding hands. Occasionally Estelle would

148

whimper and Dupree would tighten his hold on her. "Day's coming," he said. "It won't be much longer now."

"Will it be all over tomorrow?" Estelle said.

"I don't know, honey. The worse, I guess. Yes, I guess the worse before another night." He touched her hair. "Essie."

She turned toward him, her eyes luminous in the lamplight. "Would you like to go into Hunter City and take some of those night courses at that university center?" he said.

She shook her head. "I'm no good with books and studying," she said.

"You want to go back to working at the café?" he said.

"I guess. I reckon." She got up and pulled the blinds up, letting the gray light of morning into the room. Behind her Dupree switched off the lamp, leaving them in a half-lit world where the solid shapes of furniture bulked strangely in unfamiliar ways. "You think Carter's found Laura?" Estelle said.

Dupree shook his head. "I don't know," he said. "I hope so."

Estelle sighed. "I guess Julie's gone a long way by now," she said.

"A long way," Dupree said. "She'll make New Orleans before night."

On the square Jackson Ferguson stood tiredly against the Sulphur Well. He had quit making the circuit now. He was only waiting for morning to come fully so that he could go home and go to bed. He felt very tired and very old. Somewhere in the back of his mind the idea of retirement was stirring slowly, pushing its way toward the top of his mind, telling him to give the town to Thurston Marlow. He shook his head impatiently.

Arlie had told him simply and plainly in a very few words. He had walked toward him in the darkness, stopping just outside the light from the intersection so that he'd had to look out toward him into the darkness, feeling exposed, caught, vulnerable in the light. Caged.

"Father," that voice had said inexorably. The voice he recognized as somehow belonging to a boy who had walked into Bellefonte a long time ago and slept in a wagon behind a mule barn. "I've given Julie Hobson my car. She's on her way out of town in that car now. I want

149

her to make it to wherever she wants to go. I don't want my car turning up in some hick officer's report somewhere, nor in a big city police district neither. I want my car to disappear."

"Who is it?" Jackson heard himself say. "What is it?"

"You know me," Arlie said. "Just like I know you."

He had stared out, trying to see him, trying to get one look now at that face he had watched for years, at first in fear and, later, when it had become apparent that the resemblance meant nothing to anyone but him, in a kind of awe. In a living wonder that a moment of longing and involvement which he had been denying ever since had produced this boy, this man. And latterly with pride, because it was apparent that this was a man no one spoke to lightly, a man who walked quiet.

"Do you hear me?" Arlie said.

"I hear you," he said. "Do you think I'll do it?"

"I know you'll do it," Arlie said. Then he was gone. Only a lessening of darkness where a darker shade had bulked told him of the absence.

"You gone, boy?" he said softly into darkness. And when there was no answer, "Son?"

But there was only a uniform darkness and as he stepped out of the cage of light he saw that the space around him was empty of anything or anyone.

He had not finished his circuit, cutting across the square instead to stand leaning against the Sulphur Well in the coming morning. Waiting, feeling the age in him rise up like the morning light.

Arlie sat in his straight chair, tilted back against the wall of the service station. He could smell the dawn on the wind. Down the street the night light burned in the newspaper office. He stretched, feeling the lengthening of muscle in his shoulders with enjoyment. It had been a long night. He did not think of Julie now. It would have to wait. For the moment he wanted only to feel the freedom in him, the sense of well-being and ease in his body. Nothing else. Not yet.

Nothing moved on the square. He thought of Laura Lee and wondered if Carter had found her. Maybe he should go look around himself. But he thought she'd go home. Nice girls always ended up by going home. There wasn't anywhere else for them to go.

150

And out on the Chattanooga highway, far enough away from town for the houses to be thinning, far enough past Five Points so that the last of even the night people were left behind, Laura Lee stopped running.

At first she had merely run, going nowhere, thinking nothing. She had come this way because it was the easiest way to turn coming out of the café. She'd run, full tilt, out of the square and down the middle of the street, past the chiropractor's office that backed into her own yard, past the sleeping houses of North Street, past the new super-markets and the creek and into the intersection of Five Points where the lights from the filling stations and drive-ins picked her up, throwing shadows before and behind her as she ran.

Once on the highway she had run faster at first. It was a clear straight road through the darkness and there was no wind. But gradually as the road stretched on in front of her she slowed, and when she slowed her mind began to function again under the blind panic, so that gradually she ran slower and slower and knew that her heart was pounding and her mouth was dry and that she had a stitch in her side. I've been running, she thought. I've been running an awful long way. She stopped.

Around her the countryside lay blank and dark. Some-where around the next curve in the road she could see a pale glow of light, filtering through the trees from the power substation. She became aware that she was alone in the darkness on the outskirts of town.

She was afraid. But it wasn't panic any more. It was the natural fear of being alone at night on a deserted stretch of road. Her mind even gave her a cue to steer by. *It's like you used to imagine it would be if some boy actually really made you walk home. Did any boy ever really do that?* So she was able to deduce from it and reason about it, and she thought, I ought to get off the road. It's somebody coming along in a car I've got to watch out for. She stepped off the side of the highway into the ditch, then clambered out on the other side and stood in a fringe of trees along the edge of the road. Slow-ly and carefully she began walking back toward home.

After a while she couldn't concentrate on just walking and keeping out of the sight of headlights any more so that she remembered why she had been running and the fear came back to her, the shock and sudden wonder, and the hurt, an all-enveloping stabbing pain of betrayal. Walking through the darkness she tried to understand it, why it could make so much difference to her that Sonny was involved in something she couldn't understand. He was her brother, of course, and he was a remembered steady hand, but it was more than losing a brother or a prop. It was something in herself that she couldn't face. Not Sonny's defection, but some defection of her own.

She knew suddenly, thinking about it, looking at it, that she had been playing the night side as much as Sonny had. Only she hadn't admitted it to herself. She had escaped the house she lived in by running into night and Carter's arms that represented night for her. But she hadn't even had the courage to give herself to it as Sonny had done. In that way Sonny was still stronger than she was. He lived in the world she had only tried to use.

She reached an open stretch and ran across it, coming into the shelter of trees again with relief. She hurried now, feeling herself in peril, thinking of being picked up or raped or knocked in the head, and beside the sudden physical fear the terrors of the mind seemed to fall into place. Here in the fear of ending, the way that Sonny made his money didn't seem so terribly important any more. When it comes to the bare question of living or dying, other people fall into a perspective of their own. As her fear grew of being found, caught, attacked in darkness, Sonny ceased to be anything except Sonny. He wasn't a hero or a father or a steady flame of hope. He was only her older brother who had found a funny damned way to make a living. And, given Irene and her father, who could blame him too much for that? And with Sonny the night fell into perspective too. It became for her, walking through the last of it, only the other side of day.

She came that far in the darkness but she wasn't able yet to come the whole way, to take the full burden on herself. She wasn't ready yet to learn the final fact. That man is alone with himself in dark or daylight. That this is his damnation and his salvation, his freeing cross. She thought of Carter. In front of her she could see the lights of Five Points. Maybe he's at home waiting for me, she thought. For the first time then she thought of him as a man who loved her, dark or daylight, not as a place to run into the night. I'll go find him, she thought. He's waiting for me somewhere and I'm going to love him in dark or daylight because he's the one for me to love. Sonny may be gone; but Carter's always Carter, in night or morning. He'll hold me and everything will be all right.

Carter drove as far out of town as he thought Laura Lee could have possibly gone, but he saw no sign of her. The streets were empty and silent in the morning, at Five Points the few lights still on blinked wearily onto empty concrete and gravel. He turned around and drove back to town to question Dupree about her. He learned nothing. He tried to think of things Laura Lee had told him, places she might go when in trouble, somebody she might want to see. There wasn't anybody. He'd never heard her mention anyone at all.

He drove to her house and stopped the car a half block away, parking in the driveway of an apartment house. He sat for a few minutes under the wheel, looking out at the darkness, wondering what he was going to do if he found her. She didn't give a damn about him, he thought. He was nothing but an anchor to her, somewhere to go because she didn't want to be at home. He was tired of it suddenly, weary with her, weary with himself. He shut his eyes, letting the darkness swim inside him, hearing his uncle's voice talking of masks and shadows. He thought of night, the dark-enveloping, all-encompassing world he moved in, cut through by the smallest of lights, Laura Lee. And Laura Lee was nothing to see by, Laura Lee was nothing to hold onto, any more than he was. They were all a bunch of posturing fools seeking gratification from each other and finding nothing but night again.

With annoyance he felt desire stir in him, thinking that that, too, was too much to ask of anybody, the constant offering and withdrawing, the constant start and sudden abrupt unconsummated ending. He got out of the car.

To his left up the street the night light from the supermarket glowed, to his right the street lamp on the corner shone feebly. He walked down the sidewalk slowly, hearing the tap of his heels on concrete, clipping into the night with a sound of authority. He crossed the street and stood looking at Laura Lee's house. What's the matter

153

with all of us? he thought, looking at the worn steps and the gray railed porch, seeing the vines move in the wind. What the hell are we trying to find or do or be? What's Will want to hate me for? What's Julie want with Arlie when she's got to leave him? What are we all after? What are we hiding? It is because we're all afraid of something? Is it death? Or just the darkness that surrounds it? Is it the end of everything we fear, or just the night?

He walked up the wooden steps slowly, trying to be quiet, trying to move with care, wishing suddenly for Arlie's grace. He had thought she might be there in the porch swing, waiting for him, but the swing was empty, hanging from its rusty chains with a look of disuse. He crossed to the screen door.

"Laura?" he called as quietly as he could, hearing his voice whisper back at him out of the empty hallway, "Laura?"

A door opened inside. He heard it but he couldn't see anything through the screen though he strained his eyes toward the sound, hoping for a glimpse of her hair or her white dress. There was only blackness. Then the voice, speaking hoarsely and urgently out of the blackness in front of him. "Come on in here," it said.

The door opened in front of him and he walked into the hallway, not thinking at first, standing still just inside the door, still straining to see. "Laura?" he said again.

"In here," the voice said. Then there was a hand on him. He stood still, feeling the night crash around him, all the blackness and darkness and horror he knew now that night had always been to him, all the time of hate and fear of it, the lying awake while the people came and went in the kitchen beyond his bedroom; the desperate reveling in that night when he was old enough to get out into it.

He tried to think of Laura Lee, but, as always when the things of night overwhelmed him, she wasn't there. He thought instead of Essie sitting beside him in the cab, her face drawn and pale in the light from the dashboard, her body still shrinking from the handling by alien hands. He thought of Will with hate written across his face, then of his voice, hot against him on that long-ago summer evening, talking evil to him under the dusty, distant stars. He thought of Julie, driving away from Arlie back to her old commitment, and of Jackson Ferguson, walking like a ghost around the dark stone of the square.

The painted face of all the world of after-dark leered at him in the darkness. Oh, Laura, he thought, save me. But Laura's face when it finally came to him was the face of moonlight, white and cold and uninterested in an empty sky.

All right, damn it, he thought. This too then. Betray her for good and all and it will be over. Take the darkness. If it's always there waiting to trap us, go to meet it. The rest in only a mask of Halloween. In him the tiger moved, out of blackness. He felt it, watching it as he would watch a stranger though he had lived with it forever. He watched it, welcomed it, and opened the cage. He followed Irene Colvin into the dark front room . . .

Like vomiting, he thought, buttoning his pants. About as quick and about as effective. He stumbled across the room and leaned against the doorjamb. Behind him he could hear her moaning and begging him to come back. He shook his head violently, going through the doorway and into the dawn-lighted hall, hearing above her voice the snores from the upstairs bedroom. He turned toward where the open door was a lighter space in the grayness.

Laura was standing, clinging, against the front door screen. He could see her white dress, caught against the darkness of the mesh wire, her face a paler oval above the dress. He walked on toward the doorway, watching her hanging there like a giant luna moth, trapped against the wire. As he walked toward her she made a sound. He could feel the hair stand up on the back of his neck. It was like no sound he had ever heard in his life before, so lost, so alien, so unbelievable that for a moment his stunned mind tricked him and he thought she must *be* a moth, or some other nocturnal creature, thrown up against that door with still-wet wings. Out of her element. Doomed. Damned.

Then she was gone. There was only the echo of that sound and an empty doorway. He went through it into a street where day was thrusting itself bodily from the east, cold and gray and sunless, the lightening sky before the sun.

He half-stumbled down the steps, looking for her, searching up the street. Seeing her then, running again, going toward the street light on the corner, the white dress luminous in the morning. He started to run after her, was already under momentum, one foot out, when he stopped. What could he do if he caught her? It slapped at him, the hugeness and helplessness of it. There was nothing he could do. Nothing except make it worse. At least he could avoid that. He could give her the privacy in which to suffer. It was the only thing he had to give.

So he stood there, watching that white dress disappear under the street light on the corner and go on back up the highway, the highway she must have gone up once already. And come back down with hope. He'd taken that away from her. Maybe for good this time. But while he watched her disappear he wondered if that was only arrogance. What was it his uncle had said about Laura Lee? No set picture of herself yet. Maybe that would save her. He couldn't. He was too strung across the bars of salvation to understand its meaning. He went back to his car and got into it and drove onto the square.

It was dawn now. The shapes of buildings rose suddenly into being along the streets. The street lights went out.

Arlie sat on in front of the filling station, watching his street. There was no one abroad yet but soon there would be, the man with the Sunday morning papers, the postal clerk. And later the glut and swell of morning would begin, the church-goers, the merchants and doctors and lawyers, the girls in their flowered hats.

Carter's taxi turned the corner at the post office. He drove up onto the apron and stopped. Arlie slapped the chair down onto all four legs and stood up. He stretched and started across the concrete toward him. Carter got out of the car.

"Did you find Laura?" Arlie said.

"What about Julie?"

Arlie laughed. "She's all right," he said. "She's gone." He looked at Carter. "What's the matter?"

Carter shook his head.

"Laura?"

"Gone."

"Gone?"

"Yes. Forever this time. For good. Gone. For me anyway."

156

"You sure?"

Carter nodded. He walked past Arlie and sat down on the chair he had vacated. "I could use some coffee," he said. "Can we go up to your place and make some coffee?"

"Sure," Arlie said. "You need a drink?"

Carter shook his head. "You ever think about your own head, Arlie?" he said slowly. "You ever think you don't know yourself?"

"Yep," Arlie said. "Don't everybody?"

"Do they?"

"Yep."

"So how do you live with it?" Carter said.

"A day at a time . . . you know."

"Or a night?"

"Or a night."

"It's morning," Carter said.

"It's morning."

"I got to take a bath."

"All right," Arlie said. "I got a shower."

"You never ask questions, do you?"

"Nope. I figure anybody got anything to tell me they'll tell me. They usually do. If it's important anyway. Somebody always says it, sooner or later. Somebody's always got the answers." He watched Carter. "Julie said something to me before she left," he said.

Carter looked up at him, his eyes wary, troubled in the early light.

"You want to hear it?"

"All right. You said somebody always had the answers."

Arlie laughed, a short harsh sound. "She said this, Carter. She said love can stand betrayal. That's what she said to me."

"Not this kind of betrayal," Carter said.

"She didn't say the love wouldn't be changed or lost by it in a material sort of way," Arlie said. "She meant the love would last."

"Does it matter?"

"That's what she meant. It does. So that next time, next week, next month, next year, next life, it's there to build on. At least I reckon that's what she meant."

Carter stood up. "It's a nice thought," he said.

"It's all we got," Arlie said. He stood up. "How about that coffee?"

Carter followed him around the side of the building toward the stairs. "You trying to tell me," he said, "that there'll come a time when Laura Lee doesn't hate me?"

Arlie looked at him. "I don't know," he said. "But I do know this. Sometimes when what we think is the very worst happens, it frees us. Sometimes it's the only thing that can."

At the foot of the steps Carter stopped, looking out across the empty courthouse lawn, the empty streets waiting in early light. A small blonde image ran across the waste of his mind, her hair shining in sunlight. She filled his mind with sunlight, a sudden golden splash in darkness. Then she was gone. He put his foot on the first step.

"Hey, Carter."

He turned, looking down the street toward the voice. Herbert Winston was coming toward them in his half-lope. "Damn, you're hard to catch up with," he said. "I was hunting you about your uncle."

"I got the message," Carter said.

"Good. How about the money?" Herbert said.

Carter looked at him blankly.

"The taxi money," Herbert said. "You never come back and settled up. You never kicked in that twenty you was supposed to get from Dupree."

Carter stared at him. "Why . . . I reckon I never collected it," he said. "I'm sorry, Herbert. I just forgot."

"O.K.," Herbert said. "O.K. I'm just reminding you. I been sitting down there on my tail since midnight waiting on you. I reckon I can wait another few hours."

"No," Carter said. "Wait a minute." He reached in his pocket, his mind fumbling with the fares of half a lifetime ago, counting neatly, subtracting the percentage, taking the money out and handing Herbert his share. "It's all there except Dupree's," he said. "I'll get it when he opens up."

"That's all right," Herbert said. "Catch it tonight." He turned away from them. "I sure could use a little sleep," he said. "I'm draggin'." He went away down the empty street.

Arlie laughed. "You see," he said. "They ain't ever gonna give you time to sit around figuring life out. You got to keep on tallying up the take." He put his hand on Carter's

158

shoulder. "It'll all look better after a cup of coffee," he said.

"Sure," Carter said. "It always does."

The square was empty. Around the open space the buildings stood tall toward morning. The sky was blue. Jackon Ferguson walked away from the Sulphur Well across the pavement. His body loomed suddenly in the emptiness.

"There he goes," Carter said. "It's daylight."

"Yeah," Arlie said. He looked, too. "There he goes."

Jackson Ferguson turned and walked across the street toward the southeast corner, stepping carelessly on the yellow parking lines. Then he was gone and the square was empty again.

On the highway, not so far away this time, Laura Lee stopped running. She stood still watching the sky turn blue in front of her. To her left the hills rose, a darker blue thrust up from the waiting earth. She was alone. The sun was up now. There were birds singing and the wind had stopped. It was daylight. All over this side of the world.